Chance of a Lifetime

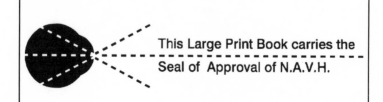

This Large Print Book carries the
Seal of Approval of N.A.V.H.

CHANCE OF A LIFETIME

KELLY EILEEN HAKE

THORNDIKE PRESS
A part of Gale, Cengage Learning

GALE
CENGAGE Learning

Detroit • New York • San Francisco • New Haven, Conn • Waterville, Maine • London

GALE
CENGAGE Learning

LIBRARY OF CONGRESS CATALOGING-IN-PUBLICATION DATA

Hake, Kelly Eileen.
    Chance of a lifetime / by Kelly Eileen Hake.
        p. cm. — (Kentucky chances ; bk. 3) (Thorndike Press large print Christian historical fiction)
    ISBN-13: 978-1-4104-0753-5 (alk. paper)
    ISBN-10: 1-4104-0753-5 (alk. paper)
    1. Large type books. I. Title.
PS3608.A54545C49 2008
813'.6—dc22   2008010367

Published in 2008 by arrangement with Barbour Publishing, Inc.

Printed in the United States of America
1 2 3 4 5 6 7 12 11 10 09 08

To my family and friends, who love and support me unconditionally.
Thank you, guys!

CHAPTER 1

1874

Billows of soot filled the air, enveloping the yard. Daisy Thales put all her disappointment, hurt, and rage into the rug beater as she walloped the smoky taint of the fire from the clothes.

Whump for Peter, her first sweetheart and loving husband, who had died from pneumonia just months before their child came into the world.

Whump for everyone who looked at her palsied son in pity. Jamie's hands and legs weren't steady, but his heart more than made up for it. She would only have him for a short time — he wasn't strong enough to live past childhood.

Whump for their home in Hawk's Fall, Kentucky, which burned to the ground a fortnight ago, leaving them with only the clothes she couldn't wash until now, because they had nothing else to wear.

She and Jamie had made it through everything life hurled at them, and she'd make sure they kept on doing so. After Peter went to his eternal reward, she'd supported herself and her son by making delicate lace for fancy ladies. She had birthed Jamie alone in their house, the pains coming too quick to fetch help. When Jamie's little legs jerked and twitched, she'd taken him to the doctor three towns over and learned her son had palsy and likely wouldn't live past his first birthday without professional medical care. Her beautiful boy would be turning five come the fall. Every time she came up against a grief greater than she thought she could survive, Daisy had plowed on ahead and made a life for herself and the son who was her one joy.

And I'll do it again. Hattie took us in after the fire, but we cain't live off her and Widow Hendrick's generosity for long. It would be so easy to stay in the warm home with Hattie's healing knowledge to help Jamie sleep through the night. But we're nothing more than charity, no matter what Hattie says about me helping with the old healer.

Daisy straightened her shoulders before whipping the clothes off the line and carrying them over to the soapy wash water.

Owin' Hattie is one thing — she's kin. But

I'm even beholden to those Chance men — complete strangers, mind. If it weren't for how Logan brung me that material to make new clothes, I couldn't have washed the old ones. We barely escaped that fire with the clothes on our backs.

She winced at the memories. Jamie had awakened her in the middle of the night, the hearth rug aflame and the fire greedily spreading to take away all they owned. She scooped him up and bolted for the door, not stopping until she was sure Jamie would be safe. Then she ran back for her lace-making basket, the only way she could eke out a living and take care of her son. She'd had the presence of mind to snatch Jamie's favorite blanket, as well. By the time she made it out, the roof was collapsing behind her. It was still hard to breathe sometimes on account of the smoke she'd taken in that night.

The fumes of the lye soap stung her eyes, and she let a few tears fall before taking the clothes and plunging them into the cool, fresh rinse water. She wrung them out, then pinned them to the clothesline to dry.

Almost good as new. Daisy nodded to herself. *And we will be, too.*

She finished the rest of the washing before going inside to start dinner. Hattie'd set out early in the morning to visit an ailing family and wouldn't be back before supper. The Chance brothers had been hard at work all day, so Daisy reckoned they'd have a hollow leg apiece to fill.

"Ma! 'Ook!" Jamie pushed his slate toward her, and she picked it up.

"That's wonderful, Jamie!" He'd copied his name from Miz Willow's spidery scrawl, and his big, wavering, loopy letters filled the slate. She handed it back to him. "Now practice it one more time."

Jamie's chalk rubbed slowly along the board while Daisy wondered whether or not to call Logan and Bryce to come in and wash up. She could still hear them sawing lumber outside while she sliced bread and put it on the table. She hastily put together a platter full of chicken sandwiches and cheese. She rang the dinner bell. That'd do. After dinner she'd start a hearty pot roast with potatoes and carrots for supper. And as a special treat, she'd bake a fresh apple pie.

Logan and Bryce deserved it for working so hard on the new addition to Willow Hendrick's house. The healer's home already had an extra room to store medicines and such, but with Hattie and Logan fixin' on marrying each other, they'd need a place of their own. Logan worked like a man with a fine reward waiting at the end of his labor, and his brother kept pace alongside him.

The two brothers walked into the cabin, and Daisy was once again struck by how much they could look so alike but be so different. Both were tall and well built, with blue eyes and brown hair. Logan, his easy smile and chin set like someone who usually got his way, stood a few inches shy of his older brother.

Daisy reckoned she'd pegged Logan Chance the first time she saw him — a good-natured, exuberant, polite young man who'd treat her sister-in-law well and give Hattie the love she deserved. Every person on earth wanted something, and Logan wanted Hattie, as well as to stay in Salt Lick Holler. By building this addition, he'd get both.

Bryce wasn't so easy to figure out. His broad shoulders and quiet manner announced to the world that he was a man who stood firm in his decisions. His smile, though much harder won than that of his brother, would break across his face like a lightning bolt and shine with an intensity that startled her. There was a calm in his deep blue eyes that made Daisy wonder what he knew that she didn't.

"Hey, buddy." Bryce's strong hands gently ruffled her son's pale blond hair.

"Hi, Byce." Jamie beamed up at the big man with all the adulation usually reserved for a boy's father. But Jamie had no father, so it would do him good to be around Logan and Bryce for a while.

If only Peter had lived, everything would be so different. . . .

Daisy pushed away the wistful thought. "If only" had to be about as useless an idea as ever existed. Stuck in the here and now, longing for the past only made each day that much harder.

Bryce straightened up and mopped his brow. He and Logan had come a long way on the addition to the main cabin, but it would still take a lot of work to complete.

It took so much less time back in California at Chance Ranch where Gideon, Daniel, Titus, and Paul were on hand to help me and Logan. Now that Logan's staying here in Salt Lick Holler, all six of us will never put our hands to the same project again.

And recently they'd worked on many projects like this one. The past five years had brought five brides — one for each of Bryce's brothers. Before Logan came to the holler and met Hattie, they'd acquired four

12

sisters-in-law back at the ranch. Miriam, the missionary's daughter, came for her sister's children and got Gideon. Alyssa, maid turned heiress, popped up mysteriously to snare Titus. Delilah, the gambler's daughter, planted herself into Paul's heart. Meanwhile, the three McPherson brothers who'd courted her simultaneously were persuaded to write back home for brides. So Eunice, Lois, and Temperance had arrived to wed Obie, Hezzy, and Mike. Lovejoy, Tempy's older sister, shepherded them all to Reliable, won a hard-fought battle for the widower Daniel's love, becoming his second wife and stepmother to Polly and Ginny Mae.

Yep. Things had gotten pretty crowded and chaotic back home, and Bryce had noticed Logan itching for some adventure. When Bryce first suggested that Logan stretch his legs and see some of the world, he hadn't planned on tagging along. All the same, he somehow got hitched to Logan's wagon. The Chance vote approving Logan's trip came with the condition that Bryce accompany his younger brother, so the two ended up in Salt Lick Holler, a tiny community carved into the Appalachian Mountains. Bryce had suggested visiting Lovejoy's hometown, never suspecting that once it

13

came time to return to California, he'd be leaving his closest brother behind.

The supper bell rang, so Bryce put away his tools and ambled into the cabin. *Something sure smells good.*

" 'Ook!" Jamie ordered, pushing a slate into Bryce's hand.

Bryce held it up in the light and saw a row of *J–a–m–i–e*s squiggling down the board in the painstaking and still shaky hand of a young boy. He nodded seriously and handed it back to Jamie before taking a seat.

"You're coming a long way, Jamie." Bryce wasn't one to scoop out handfuls of praise. He figured an honest assessment would go further than ebullience. Besides, Jamie deserved to be treated with the dignity befitting a man. Even if he was young, the boy had more inner strength than just about anyone Bryce had ever met. It looked like Jamie got that from his mama. She'd been through a lot of tough times — too many, to Bryce's way of thinking — but she still had a smile for her son and anyone else who needed encouragement. Bryce admired them both.

He sneaked a surreptitious glance at Daisy as she poured fresh milk into her son's cup. A petite woman, her generous curves and loving smile lent her an unconventional beauty — the beauty of a woman rather than the untested prettiness she undoubtedly possessed as a young girl. Her long, honey-colored hair hung past her waist. Not a single lock dared to break free. She braided her hair in an intricate pattern similar to the woven reins he used when training a horse. He wondered what she'd look like when it came unraveled, her hair shining in waves to frame her big brown eyes and the smattering of freckles across her sun-kissed nose.

She turned around, and a puzzled look crossed her face when he was too slow to hide his gaze. Bryce cleared his throat.

"Ahem. Could I have some of that?" He stuck out his empty cup. Never mind the fact that he didn't like milk — he drained the glass by the end of the meal, since she'd smiled so pretty when she filled it for him.

Miz Willow — Bryce had to keep reminding himself to call her that instead of Widow Hendrick, since Hattie'd told him that the older woman preferred those who lived in her home to call her by that name — chatted with Logan and Daisy, but he didn't see any reason to join in. Why speak up if he didn't have something to contribute? He mostly got by with *yes, nope,* or a good

15

shrug. Sometimes he wished he had a little more to add and Logan a little less.

Bryce ate his sandwiches silently, listening to the others, and nodding his head occasionally as the conversation required. He noticed Jamie eyeing the sliced cheese. The little tyke was too polite to interrupt the adults to ask for some more. Bryce winked at Jamie as he pushed the plate close enough for him to choose a piece. The little boy's smile — so full of joy and gratitude — warmed Bryce's heart as he and Logan left and got back to work.

"Hand me more nails. I ran out," Logan directed from up the makeshift ladder, where he was hammering together the frame of the first wall.

Bryce, holding the base, rummaged through his pockets until he gathered a fistful, then offered them to his brother. He squinted as Logan pounded the nails in and joined the frame to the pre-existing wall of the cabin. Then Logan jumped down, and Bryce clambered up to make sure the lines were even — it was always best to double-check these sorts of things.

"We're fine." Bryce came back down and walked over to the pile of lumber. He picked out another piece of wood to saw down to a small piece. The tiny bar, when wedged and secured between the two bigger pieces forming the corner, would support the wall and make it stronger.

"Lumber pile's getting low," Logan observed.

"Yep." Bryce finished his sawing.

"We should go fill up the wagon with another load from the barn and bring it over." Logan shifted his weight from one foot to the other, eager to build Hattie their new home. "Are you done with that yet?"

"Yep." Bryce nodded his head and jumped back down beside his brother. "You know that getting something done quick and getting something done right don't always go together."

"Yeah," Logan grumbled and picked up the pace. "I can only take one thing slow at a time. The wedding's already waiting!"

Bryce grinned. He'd spoken his piece, and Logan had heard him. That would be good enough. They'd been working steadily since dinner, but now the sunlight was failing. After they moved this load, he and Logan would be done working on the cabin for today. One more week and it would be finished.

He saw Daisy come out of the house with a basket on her hip, walking over to the clothesline. The setting sun caught the fire

17

in her hair, surrounding her face with a golden halo. Bryce drank in the sight. *She's the closest thing to an angel I'll ever see.*

CHAPTER 2

"Today's your big day, Hattie!" Daisy gestured to the old wooden tub, which she'd already filled with warm water. "I've drawn you a bath." Jamie snoozed in the big bed.

"Thankee, Daisy." Hattie slid the screen in place and disappeared behind it, only the soft splash of water marking her presence.

"While yore in there, Miz Willow's taking some breakfast out to the barn for your groom and his brother." Daisy put the cinnamon rolls in the ash oven to keep warm. "Silk Trevor's already at the school-house, making shore it's neat and tidy." Daisy didn't tell Hattie how Silk and the women of the community had gotten together to decorate the schoolhouse with flowers. A bride deserved to have a surprise on her wedding day.

"It's so kind of them!" Daisy could hear the smile in Hattie's voice.

"When yore finished in there, don't

19

dawdle." Daisy forced herself to be strict. "We've still got lots to do this morning, and you haven't et so much as a single bite."

"Oh, I don't think I cain eat a bite," Hattie demurred. "I'm too nervous."

"Nonsense." Miz Willow came in and banged the door shut. "Yore a healer — you have to have a strong stomach. Comes with the job."

"You've been married once before," Daisy encouraged. "You know how the ceremony will go. He waits for you, Otis Nye escorts you to him, and then you both say, 'I do.' " The words carried her back to the happiest day in her life. Daisy had stood all in white, with flowers woven into her hair as she promised to love Peter for as long as they lived. . . .

Why did it have to be such a short time? We didn't even have a single full year together as man and wife.

No. I cain't think about that now. It's Hattie's day. She deserves to be happy, especially after how hard her first marriage to Peter's brother was. She never uttered a single word of complaint but waited on Horace hand and foot for precious little thanks.

"Let me do that for you." Daisy took the towel from Hattie's hands and sat her down by the fire so her hair would dry more quickly. Hattie had wisely donned her yellow dress instead of the green one she'd chosen to wear for the ceremony.

"You have such lovely color," Daisy murmured as she rubbed Hattie's hair, combing through it before toweling it again. The deep mahogany of her damp locks slowly gave way to burnished copper. "We've all decided you cain't wear it back in a braid on yore weddin' day," Daisy spoke firmly over Hattie's tiny squeak of dismay. "And none of those awful buns where yore head looks scraped back, neither."

"What are you going to do?" Hattie moved restlessly as Daisy gathered up a few locks and began to weave them in a pretty fishtail pattern.

"Yore jist gonna hafta trust me." Daisy finished the first plait, then made another of the same kind on the other side of Hattie's head, joining them together in the back with a pretty green ribbon. The joined braids were fitting for a bride, and they seemed almost to form a crown atop the rest of her hair, which hung in loose waves past her waist. Daisy coaxed a few wispy tendrils to curl alongside Hattie's face and let it be. "There. That'll do."

Hattie got up and headed for the mirror to inspect her new hairstyle. She peered at herself from a few angles and sighed in satisfaction.

"I don't know how you did it, Daisy, but you made me look almost young again!" Hattie rushed over and wrapped her in a hug. "Thankee!"

"You are young," Miz Willow piped up. Her face softened. "But I'll allow as how nice you look with the way Daisy done yore hair."

"Jamie, time to git dressed!" Daisy began laying out his new clothes.

"You should do yore hair jist like this," Hattie begged.

"It ain't fittin' for the matron of honor," Daisy protested. *Matron, and me practically the same age as the bride.*

"Yore not weaselin' out of this. Today is the last day for the Thales sisters to be all done up like each other." Hattie took Daisy's hands in hers. "I want you to share this with me, Daisy."

"I cain't say no to that." Daisy gave in before helping Jamie into his Sunday best.

"Good." Hattie went over to put on her wedding dress, a light grass green that set off her hair and creamy skin.

Daisy pulled Jamie's shirt on over his head and began to comb his hair, pretending to be completely engrossed in what she was doing as she heard Hattie's gasp.

"Daisy! When did you . . . ?" She fingered the delicate handmade lace collar adorning her wedding dress.

"It's what I do, darlin'!" Daisy smiled at the look on Hattie's face, glad she'd decided to give her one of the lacy collars she made to sell in fancy shops. "I'm jist glad you like it."

Jamie and I coulda used that money, but good friends are worth more'n gold, and Hattie's the best there is. She deserves to feel as beautiful as God made her, and I may not have much to my name right now, but I could give her this.

"It's beautiful, Daisy!" Hattie slipped into the dress and went over to show Miz Willow. "I don't know how you do it!" Her face changed as she looked into Daisy's eyes. "Thankee."

"Yore welcome, Hattie." Daisy squeezed her friend's hand. "I hope today is as special and full of love as yore marriage will be." *And as mine was.*

"Hold still, Logan!" Bryce gritted, trying to make sense of Logan's necktie. "You're jumpier'n a frog."

"Sorry, Bryce." Logan looked anything but sorry. He had a grin as big as all get-out on his face. "I'm excited. Today I take Hattie to be my wife."

"I'm gaining another fine sister-in-law," Bryce agreed, taking the ends of his brother's tie once more. Between their efforts, they'd already crumpled the thing past all hope. Somehow Bryce managed to finally work it into a presentable shape.

"And Louisville for our honeymoon — have you seen how excited Hattie is about buying new books for the schoolhouse?" Logan buffed his boots one last time.

"Yep." Bryce ran a comb through his hair. "Who would've thought when I told you to visit Salt Lick Holler that you'd find yourself a bride — much less one who'd found a hidden box of money while cleaning out the loft for us?"

"Lovejoy's first husband must've been quite a clench fist to squirrel away seventy dollars and hide it up in the barn," Logan mused. "Sure was nice of her to give Miz Willow her old home and even better that she trusted me to spend the money on helping the holler."

"Just who she is," Bryce observed. Lovejoy Spencer had been Willow Hendrick's protégée and the main healer for Salt Lick Holler before coming to California with the new brides and had wound up finding a husband

24

of her own in surly old Daniel. She'd worked wonders for their brother back at Chance Ranch and made a good mother to his children, Polly and Ginny Mae.

If it weren't for Lovejoy Spencer and the McPherson family, Bryce never would have suggested this trip. As it was, the whole thing had taken a lot of unexpected turns — like how the whole family insisted that Bryce go along. And now Logan was getting married and leaving Bryce behind at Salt Lick Holler while he took his honeymoon trip!

"Funny how things work out." Bryce shook his head.

"Are you sure you're okay with staying here until we get back?" Logan peered at him anxiously.

"Yep," Bryce hastened to reassure his brother. "Besides, I'll chop enough wood to last you through winter. You could use some more meat in the smokehouse, too, so I'll be hunting and fishing. I'll have plenty to keep me busy until you get back."

A soft melody floated through the air as Hattie began to walk down the aisle. Bryce stood beside his brother and watched. The duties of the best man were few on the surface — stand by and encourage the

25

groom — but deeper truth lay beneath. Today, for the last time, Bryce would be the closest friend to his brother, and for the first time, he would watch as someone else became the most important person in Logan's life.

Now Hattie would help him, love him, make a home with him, and share the days they were given — as it should be. A man should leave home and cleave to his wife. But Bryce didn't look forward to going back home. Chance Ranch wouldn't be the same without his younger brother, who always understood what Bryce couldn't find the words to say.

As Logan looked at his bride, Bryce watched him. His baby brother — the only one younger than Bryce — had grown up right before his eyes. His brother, the scapegrace who managed to find mischief and fun as though he had a compass for it, stood straight and tall, with the love in his heart shining from his face. Coming to Salt Lick Holler had made a man out of the boy, and Bryce had to admit that Hattie had a lot to do with it. She would be a good wife to him, and Logan would be a devoted husband for her.

They exchanged *I do*s, and Bryce snapped out of his reverie. That did it.

Six brothers, but with Logan hitched, I'm the last Chance bachelor.

CHAPTER 3

As the entire holler and some folks from neighboring Hawk's Fall sat down to enjoy the wedding feast, Daisy led Jamie to the far end of the tables in one long row for the occasion. She'd love to sit in the middle of the banquet across from Logan and Hattie, but Jamie needed as much space as she could give him. His jerky movements would distract and discomfort others if he sat in the midst of the goings-on. She took the very edge of the bench and lifted him next to her — she couldn't take the risk that he'd tumble off the end.

When Logan and Hattie took places across the table from her, she looked up in surprise. Customarily, the newlyweds sat at the center of the table, surrounded by well-wishers. As Bryce escorted Miz Willow over, getting the old healer situated, Daisy shot Hattie a questioning look.

"It's our wedding," Hattie murmured,

positively glowing.

"We'll sit at the head of our table, with our closest loved ones," Logan finished. "No one will gainsay us."

"Hey, buddy." Bryce came and took the spot on Jamie's other side.

" 'Ey, Byce!" Jamie squirmed excitedly.

"Easy, there." Bryce reached out to steady Jamie when he leaned back a little too far.

Daisy shot him a grateful smile, but Bryce only gave her a brief nod before bowing his head for the prayer. She'd never before met a man of so few words. *What goes on in that quiet head of his? Mayhap without his brother around to talk for the pair of 'em, Bryce'll speak up, and I'll learn more about him. Any man Jamie spends so much time with is someone I need to get to know.*

Soon enough, nothing more than crumbs dusted the tables, and it was time to get things moving. Silk Trevor gave Daisy a decisive nod.

"I need to go holp Silk for a minute," Daisy leaned over and whispered to Miz Willow. "Would you mind Jamie for a while?"

"No problem." Bryce Chance stood up and swung Jamie in the air.

"I —" Daisy's heart caught in her throat as Jamie squealed with the fun of falling

29

back down. She couldn't breathe for a few minutes even after Bryce caught him easily.

Doesn't the man realize Jamie's condition? Was Bryce so oblivious he didn't know Jamie needed special care?

One look at the delighted surprise on her baby boy's face and the words died on her lips. Bryce wasn't about to drop Jamie — she needed to stop overreacting. Daisy took a deep breath and joined Silk, while Bryce carried Jamie and walked with Miz Willow to the circle that was forming.

Everybody gathered around Logan and Hattie to watch them open their wedding gifts. Daisy and Silk waited for the chatter to die down before handing the first package to the happy couple.

"Wait a minute!" Rooster Linden stood up. "I got summat to say. Firstly, my gift for the happy couple is up at my place. It's a new buckboard, only I ain't got a horse to pull it down here jist yet, on account of loanin' her to a friend in need." He grinned, then sobered. "Second, and more important, I want to say in front of everybody here how grateful I am to Hattie, Logan, and Bryce Chance. They saw me through a time when I had to fight my demons. I wouldn't have pulled through if it weren't for them. Yore fine folks, and I'm glad to have Logan

30

stayin' in the holler. I'm shore I ain't the only one who feels that way." He paused while cheers erupted all around.

"Because of their holp and yore prayers, I've stopped drinkin' likker. I know I ain't the only man in this holler who owes you a 'thankee,' but it comes from the bottom of my heart. I wish you two a long and happy marriage!" With that, he sat back down, and the gift giving could truly begin. Logan ripped open the first package.

"Beautiful workmanship," he praised, running his hands over the graceful curves of hand-carved swan-neck towel pegs.

"I thought they'd look good on the wall of yore new home." Asa Pleasant spoke modestly but beamed at their pleasure.

"I expect so," Logan agreed.

Hattie opened the next gift, a full set of towels, embroidered by Silk Trevor.

"These're lovely, Silk!" She held up the corner of a wash-cloth and traced the delicate blue *C* adorning the corner.

"We'll be sure to hang them on our washstand," Logan planned aloud as he opened a bundle.

"That thar's an ole family recipe fer pickled pigs' feet." Her husband nowhere in sight, Bethilda Cleary spoke loudly as Hattie picked up a card from the baking dish.

"Ain't nobody makes it better'n my daughters, Lily and Lark, but you cain't go wrong with that thar recipe." Having spoken her piece, Bethilda sat back down.

"Thankee, Bethilda." Hattie put the cookware to the side as Logan accepted another parcel.

"I hope you like it." Abigail Rucker shifted her new baby to her shoulder while her husband, Nate, the holler's hulking blacksmith, rubbed her back between her shoulder blades.

Logan unfurled a braided hearth rug in varying shades of blue cloth.

"When did you ever find the time to make this, Abby?" Hattie stroked the pretty rug.

"Bitty Nate here don't let me sleep much anyhow." Abby blushed with pleasure. "I started it as soon as y'all tole me 'bout yore engagement."

"So did I." Cantankerous old Otis Nye shuffled forward with a large object covered by an old sheet. He set it before the newlyweds and backed up, waiting for them to reveal what he'd made.

Logan gave the sheet a short tug. It slid to the ground, revealing a maple wedding chest.

"Ooh," Hattie breathed, reaching out to touch the flowers chiseled into the wood.

32

Otis had carved blooming vines to encircle the smooth wooden sides of the chest.

"Figgured it were fittin' since yore our healer, Hattie." The old man spoke gruffly, but everyone knew he couldn't discount the time and care he'd put into his gift. "And Logan here's the one who's got me carvin' all the time now anyway."

"That's right." Logan walked over and clapped the old man on the back. "Jack Tarhill back in Louisville is gearing up for that next shipment of yours. He's very pleased with how things are working out with your and Asa's carving. Those checker sets and nativities sell very well."

"Of course they do!" Otis drew himself up and broke into a grin.

Hattie opened the next package, drawing out a beautiful blue and green wedding ring quilt.

"Miz Willow, you shouldn't have!" She fingered the thick fabric. "This belonged to yore ma."

"The good Lord didn't see fit to give me a child of my flesh." The old woman's eyes glistened. "But yore the daughter of my heart, Hattie. I figgured the time's come to pass it on."

Hattie handed Logan the quilt before rushing over to the old widow and enveloping her in a tight hug.

Ma gave me a quilt like that on Peter's and my weddin' day. Daisy blinked back tears of loss. *It burned in the fire, and now I don't have anything to remember her by.*

Women started to gather up the dishes left over from the feast. A lot of folks had a bit of a walk before they got back home, and the celebration had stretched through the afternoon. The time had come to get home to waiting chores.

Daisy slung Jamie on her hip and gathered the now-empty dishes she'd brought for the celebration. Miz Willow leaned on her cane as she hobbled on the path. Logan carried the swan-neck towel pegs and the hearth rug, while Hattie cradled their monogrammed linens. Bryce walked a bit behind, his arms full with the new wedding chest. He'd seen to it that the quilt rested inside.

After putting the bounty in Hattie and Logan's new home, Bryce retired to the barn loft where he and Logan had slept since arriving in Salt Lick Holler. He tossed his boots on Logan's empty pallet before bunking down.

At least I'll get a good night's sleep without Logan's yammering.

■ ■ ■ ■

"Hope you have a fine time," Miz Willow called after them as Logan and Hattie departed for the train station early the next morning.

"Good-bye!" Daisy waved.

From her arms, Jamie clapped his hands and let out a slightly garbled "Bye!"

"See you in two weeks." Bryce supported Miz Willow's elbow out in the yard. It seemed only fitting to give the newlyweds a proper send-off.

Once the happy couple disappeared around the bend, Daisy and Jamie trailed into the house behind Miz Willow — probably to clean up after their hasty breakfast. Bryce headed for the barn. He grabbed the milking pail and set the three-legged stool beside the cow.

"Mornin', Starla." He gave her a pat on the rump before he set about the business at hand. When the pail was full, he went out to the well and drew up last night's cold milk to exchange for the fresh. Before he and Logan had arrived, this well was the only way Hattie and Miz Willow could draw water. Now that he and Logan had installed a new water pump and piping, the well could be used strictly to keep things fresh and cool. He picked it up and headed for the cabin.

"Here you go." He plunked the pail down on the table.

"Thankee, Bryce." Miz Willow made her way across the room. "I'm fixin' to do some baking today."

Bryce looked around. Daisy busily swiped a rag around the furniture, keeping everything spick-and-span. Jamie sat on his pallet, stacking blocks. Bryce hunkered down to look the boy in the eye.

"What do you say you come and help me gather eggs this morning, Jamie?"

"Ma?" he questioned his mother before answering.

Bryce saw Daisy hesitate and could practically hear the thoughts running through her mind. *What if the chickens scratch her son or, worse, peck him?* He hadn't missed the panicked look on her face the day before when he'd tossed Jamie into the air.

"I'll hold him," Bryce reassured her. "Jamie can help me hang on to the basket." It would do the little tyke good to do something other than play with blocks and study. Jamie's legs were twisted and jerky, but he had a lot more control over his hands and arms.

"All right," she assented with a slow nod. Jamie mimicked the motion, nodding eagerly and stretching up his arms.

Bryce scooped him up, handed the boy the egg basket, and tromped back to the barn. Jamie sat in the crook of his left arm, cradling the basket as Bryce opened the chicken coop.

"You have to be real quiet so you don't startle them," Bryce explained. "Then you reach under them, nice and gentle, to see if there's an egg." He spoke the instructions as he found the first egg. "Then we put it in the basket. Want to help with the next one?"

" 'Es." Jamie nodded somberly.

"Good." Bryce took the basket and looped it over his arm, then guided Jamie's hand into the next nest.

Jamie stroked the feathers of one of the birds. His touch was clumsy but gentle.

Bryce helped the little boy reach under the chicken and find the egg. "Feel that?"

" 'Es," he whispered excitedly, his little hand closing around the egg and tugging it free.

"Good job," Bryce praised as he steadied Jamie's arm so he could place the egg in the basket.

The job took far more time than usual, but Bryce enjoyed the look of wonder and excitement on the little boy's face. If something as simple as gathering eggs could make the lad feel included, Bryce would make sure to find other things the boy could do. He carried the child and eggs back into the house.

"We're all done." Bryce transferred Jamie to Daisy's arms, then set the eggs on the table. "Eleven of 'em."

"Did you have fun?" Daisy cuddled her son close.

"None boken," Jamie declared proudly.

"That's right. Jamie was a big help. The chickens like him."

"That's my little man!" At the grin on her son's face, Daisy broke into a matching smile.

When she turned the full force of that smile onto Bryce, he almost stepped back from the impact. Daisy's brown eyes positively shone with the joy she found in her son. Bryce always knew she was attractive, but when she glowed with love, Daisy became the most beautiful woman he'd ever seen.

Bryce headed for the door. "I've got some things to tend to." He winced at how abrupt he sounded, but it couldn't be helped. He'd hardly taken a step when he felt a soft hand on his arm.

"Thankee." Daisy smiled up at him with gratitude and happiness. The warmth of her smile and the heat of her palm on his arm sparked something in him.

"Welcome," Bryce responded gruffly before retreating to the safety of the barn, where he always knew what to do.

Lord, I can understand what to do with a horse or any other creature — how to put 'em at ease. So why am I at such a loss with the pretty little widow with her heartfelt smile?

CHAPTER 4

If I didn't know any better, I'd think that man got flustered when I thanked him, Daisy mused as Bryce disappeared from view. *He's one of those men who likes to do for others but doesn't know how to handle the appreciation afterwards. It's sweet — jist like the way he treats Jamie. It's mighty nice of him to take an interest in my boy while he's here. Jamie'll never know his pa, but he cain relish bein' 'round a man like Bryce, even iff'n 'tis for but a brief time.*

Well, if he won't take an honest thankee I'll jist find another way to show my appreciation. Daisy thought for a moment before remembering the way Bryce tucked into the apple pie she'd made last month. *I reckon he's got a sweet tooth to match his nature. I'll whip up some pudding for dessert today. He oughta enjoy that. Besides, it's one of Jamie's favorites.*

With her mind made up, Daisy left Miz

Willow teaching Jamie his letters and walked into Logan and Hattie's cabin. Her closest friend hadn't had the time to settle into the home her man made for her before being whisked off to Louisville. *By the time Hattie and Logan get back,* Daisy determined, *their cabin'll be all fixed up and ready to be a home.*

She rolled up her sleeves and set to work. The addition wasn't overly large, but it didn't need to be. The cooking would still be done in the main cabin, and Logan married Hattie knowing full well she couldn't bear any children. For the two of them, the cozy room would be a perfect fit.

A harp-backed washstand with a single drawer and small cupboard sat beneath a goodly sized window, where the sunlight would warm the wash water a bit. Another wall boasted a modest fireplace to heat the room. Logan's new desk butted up against the third wall, and a real, above-the-ground bed nestled up to the wall this room shared with the main cabin.

But the pile of wedding gifts lay in the corner, waiting to put the finishing touches on the home. Daisy walked over and found the swan-neck clothing pegs. *These should be hung by the hearth, with winter coming on. Jist not too close.* She shuddered at the memory of the fire before straightening her shoulders. She walked out to the barn to find a hammer and ran into Bryce.

"Howdy." The big man took a step back.

"Hello. I'm lookin' for a hammer and some nails." Daisy peered around the barn. "Any idea where I cain find 'em?"

Bryce nodded, walked to a far corner, and returned in a minute with the requested tools. He held them out to her wordlessly, and Daisy accepted them.

I cain't make him talk to me, she reasoned, *but maybe iff'n I speak first, he'll come 'round.*

"You and yore brother made a fine home for Hattie." Daisy smiled as she spoke. "I'm gonna fix it up a bit so it's ready when they get back."

"Needs a woman's touch," Bryce agreed.

" 'Zactly." Daisy breathed a sigh of relief that Bryce didn't actually seem to mind talking to her — he just needed to be drawn out a little. "Hattie'd have it done in a trice, but she's off to Louisville, so I figgured I'd put away the weddin' gifts and get 'em all set up."

"Mighty thoughtful of you." Bryce rubbed the back of his neck as if puzzling over something. "What're the hammer and nails for?"

"The swan-neck wall hooks need to be hung." Daisy laughed. "I cain only hope I get 'em up straight."

"I'll do it," Bryce offered. "I've just finished the mantelpiece and need to put it up anyway."

"Makes sense to me." Daisy passed the hammer back to him, pleased at the progress she'd made. Bryce wasn't much of a talker, but that was all right. He went out of his way to do nice things for the people she cared about, so Daisy didn't mind making the extra effort to put him at ease.

The rest of the morning passed quickly as Daisy and Bryce worked together inside the cabin. Neither spoke much. It was enough to be working alongside each other.

While he made tiny pencil marks on the wall, determining where to hang the pegs, she carefully folded the monogrammed towels and hung them across the top of the wooden washstand. The monogrammed *C* in the corner of each towel marched across the row, each one a little higher than the last.

"They don't have a mirror," she noted. She didn't realize she'd spoken aloud until Bryce stopped hammering.

"You think they need one?" Bryce's words could've been a question or just a flat statement.

"Of course!" Daisy decided to treat it as if

it were a question. *Men!* "How else do you get yoreself ready for the day? What about yore hair?"

"Not that complicated." Bryce ran a hand through his wavy brown hair, mussing it up just enough to make Daisy itch to tug it back in place.

"Maybe not for you," she admitted, "but what about Hattie? Or," she added triumphantly, "Logan shaving?"

"We don't have a mirror out in the barn." Bryce rubbed his jaw with his big, strong hand. "We do it by feel."

Daisy's mouth went dry. *By the end of the day, Bryce's jaw boasted a dark shadow, making him look a little rugged — like he needed a good woman.* She couldn't think of a single thing that was fitting to say, so she just shrugged.

"Those hooks look wondrous fine!" He'd put four of them in a neat row by the hearth, and the other two were thoughtfully stationed beside the door.

Bryce jerked a thumb toward the latter. "I thought it'd be nice for when Hattie comes in after healing, to hang her cloak." He smirked. "And then there's one for Logan's hat."

"His and hers," Daisy mused. "Perfect."

Bryce got to work on the mantelpiece he and Logan had sanded together. With supportive legs along either side of the hearth to brace it, the subtle curves of the mantel wouldn't overpower the wall but would look like a natural part of the room.

While he worked, he watched Daisy from the corner of his eye. She bustled around contentedly, plumping a pillow here, then tucking in the edges of the wedding quilt she brought out of Hattie and Logan's new chest and put on the bed. He caught her trying to scooch the chest across the floor.

"Here." He picked the wooden chest up off the ground just as she was ready to give it another hefty push. A few flaxen tendrils of hair had escaped her fancy updo, and Bryce had a sudden picture of her brushing her hair, the golden locks spread over her shoulders. He decided to get that mirror she'd been talking about. Their eyes locked, and Bryce felt the breath hitch in his chest.

A sudden gust of air banged the door shut, breaking the moment. Daisy shook her head as though to clear it, then pointed to the far wall. "I was fixin' to put it at the foot of the bed."

Bryce tromped over and obligingly lowered the carved trunk in place. He stepped back to where he'd been working on the mantelpiece.

"Thankee, Bryce." Her words were so soft, he almost thought he imagined them.

And why wouldn't she be hesitant to thank you after the way you jackrabbited out of the house this morning? he scolded himself. *Say something this time!*

"Anytime." He forced a smile. "You could've just asked for help, Daisy." Her name tasted sweet as he spoke it.

"I would've gotten it there." Daisy's shoulders straightened, and she poked her chin out. "Women aren't helpless."

Now you've done it. You offended her. Bryce gave himself a mental kick. "I never thought you were helpless." He searched for the words. "You're a strong woman, supporting yourself and your son. I just meant you don't always have to do everything alone."

"You're right." She softened a bit and rewarded him with an apologetic smile.

Bryce grinned in return before turning back to the mantel. He finished up while she straightened the blue gingham curtains. He stepped back to survey their handiwork.

Everything stood in place, as it had when they'd started, but now it looked . . . nice.

46

Inviting. She'd looped the curtains along the wooden bar to make them flutter prettily at the window. The chest looked at home at the foot of the bed, where the quilt fell in neat folds just shy of the floor.

"The mantelpiece fits real good," Daisy commented. "All the wood — the walls, the hooks, the furniture — it melds together nice." She stepped over to the chest and drew out the braided hearth rug. After she laid it out, she stepped back to see the effect. "Blue rug, blue curtains, blue embroidery on the towels — even blue in the quilt. All looks put together jist right, with a lot of love."

That was it exactly. She'd found a way to say what he'd been thinking. The colors and goodwill made the room pleasant. Everything in here fit, just like Hattie and Logan matched each other.

"Yep."

Bryce rolled over for the umpteenth time. He couldn't sleep. It was just too . . . quiet.

Now he understood what those fancy writers meant when they wrote about the "deafening silence." The lack of sound pushed in on him and stifled all thoughts of anything else.

The din of all the Chance children surrounded him back on the ranch, and here he'd had Logan's jabber — or snoring — to put up with. Even today when he'd worked with Daisy, she hummed under her breath.

He smiled at the memory of how she didn't follow any particular tune, just made the happy noise of busyness. He'd noticed she did the same thing in the evenings while she worked over her lace. Humming came as naturally to Daisy as buzzing came to bees. Same as smiling came to Jamie. Except for when the boy bent over his studies or something requiring his absolute focus, he expressed joy. No one came closer to being a breathing sunbeam than Jamie when that bright smile spread across his face and into the heart of its recipient.

Bryce rested his head on his hands, leaning back to stare at the sloping ceiling of the loft. The lad possessed an eager young mind. He thirsted to learn about the world around him and to help those he lived with.

The eggs are a good start, Bryce decided. *Tomorrow I'll see if I can't find something more to show him. Just because he can't walk doesn't mean he can't enjoy learning how to do other things.*

A thought seeped into his mind. *It might take some smooth talking, but when the time is right, I'm going to convince Jamie's pretty mama to let me teach him how to ride. It'll give the boy something to look forward to and a way to increase his strength. After all, tending to animals is the best way I know to work the muscles and the mind.*

CHAPTER 5

A few days later, Bryce woke up early. He tended to the cow, mucked out the stalls, and gathered the eggs. He and Jamie had made egg gathering into a sort of morning ritual, but today Bryce needed to have everything squared away before breakfast.

He gave the door a cautious tap rather than walking in unannounced.

"Come on in," Daisy's cheerful voice called.

He opened the door and sniffed appreciatively. Coffee cake — one of his favorite breakfasts, but not rib sticking enough for every day.

"You're up and about a little earlier this morning," Daisy observed, pouring him a cup of coffee.

"I've got business to tend to." Bryce took a long, appreciative drink. "I'm going out to Hawk's Fall to pick up Logan and Hattie's wedding present. I won't be back until tomorrow." He waited to see her reaction.

"I see." Her words didn't match her expression. She seemed a bit confused, a little lost.

Will she miss me? Bryce shrugged the thought away. "It won't be long, but I have to go. I'm borrowing the new wagon to haul it in — it's from the whole Chance family."

"It's big enough to need a wagon?" Daisy's deep brown eyes burned with curiosity, though she was too polite to come out and ask what the present was.

"Yep." Bryce wouldn't tell her anything more. Sooner or later she'd have to learn to ask for the things she wanted, even if it was just harmless information.

"Does Miz Willow know?" Daisy changed tack, and Bryce suddenly remembered that the elderly healer had spent the night with the Peasleys, where a baby's cough caused her some worry.

"I spoke with her about how I'd need to fetch the present when it came in," he assured her. "I trust you to pass on the message."

"Let me pack you some lunch before you go," Daisy offered.

"Thanks, but I've eaten more than enough of this wonderful cake to tide me over. I'll be spending the night with Abner McPherson, and he'll expect me to bring my appetite."

"Fair enough," Daisy conceded. "Have a safe trip, Bryce. Good-bye."

His ears all but perked up at the sound of his name on her lips. She didn't say it often, so when she did, it sounded special.

"I'll be back as soon as I can," Bryce promised, swiping one last bite of coffee cake before standing up. *I plan on sticking around for a while yet.*

Out in the garden, Daisy plucked weeds as she sorted her thoughts.

"He's only going to be gone for two days — less, even," Daisy muttered to herself. "What am I doin' gettin' all het up about it? It's not like I have to be afeared of livin' without a man — it's all I've done for the past four and a half years. Me an' Jamie'll be jist fine, and I still have Miz Willow's company."

Daisy reached for a scraggly weed and plucked one of Miz Willow's yarbs out clear to the roots. She hastily replanted it and continued her musings.

What do I care iff'n Bryce Chance didn't want to tell me what he was goin' to fetch? It ain't like he's trying to be mysterious. He's just naturally tight-lipped. He's so quiet; I

52

reckon I'll hardly even notice he's not around.

Daisy's thoughts ground to a halt as she acknowledged the falsehood of that last one. She sat back on her heels and rubbed the nape of her neck.

True, Bryce was quiet, but it was hard not to notice him. The man had a presence that seemed to command her respect. He didn't need words to make his opinion known — the way he stood or even shrugged spoke volumes.

Jamie'll miss him. Jamie always notices even when people simply aren't feeling their best. Bryce didn't wake him to let him know he won't be around for a couple days.

Jamie'd looked around for Bryce at breakfast and asked her, "When go holp Byce wit eggs?"

"Not for a coupla days, Jamie." Daisy couldn't read the look in her son's eyes. "Bryce has to be gone for a while, but he'll come back soon. He has to fetch something for Hattie and Logan."

After the initial surprise, Jamie had thought for a moment.

His "oh" came out so serious it near broke my heart. But what do I expect? Bryce doesn't owe me and Jamie anything. Shore, he's spending time with us now, but we all know it won't last. As soon as I've made enough lace,

53

I can get us back to our land and rebuild a roof o'er our heads. It won't be as nice as the one before, but it'll do, and we won't be beholden to Hattie and Miz Willow no more.

It would take a long time — probably all through the winter months — to make enough lace. Logan would stay in the holler with his new bride, but Bryce hadn't made his plans to go back to California any kind of secret.

Yes, the more I think of it, the better this is. It'll get Jamie used to the idea of his friend leavin' for good. It's nice to have Bryce around, but we can't rely on him forever. She tugged hard on one particularly stubborn weed. *We don't need to. I can take care of us myself.*

The weed snapped from its roots, the sudden lack of resistance toppling Daisy backward. She scrambled up and stared at the scraggly mess of leaves.

"Stubborn thing," she muttered, shaking her head. "Don't you know when to let go, and when to hold on?"

"Hold it steady, right there," Daisy directed.

"Got 't!" Jamie's brow furrowed as he held the dustpan steady.

Daisy moved the pile of dirt from the wooden floor to the dustpan with one swift, short stroke. This was the only house she'd ever been in with real floorboards. She could sweep these, scrub them, keep them nice and clean for Jamie. That way, Jamie wouldn't get so dirty when he scooched around the house. It also gave him a steady surface to stack his blocks in complicated piles.

"Perfect!" Daisy lifted the dustpan victoriously, and Jamie clapped as she went outside to empty it. Popping back a moment later, she tickled his tummy. "Yore such a good helper, Jamie. Thankee."

"We good teeaa . . ." Jamie took a breath and tried the difficult word again. "Tee-aamm."

I wonder where he heard that? Daisy passed her hands through his soft blond hair. "We do make a fine team."

"Byce say so." Jamie smiled up at her.

"Ah." *That explains it.*

"Do t'gether," Jamie recited carefully, "wurk dun better."

"Yore a big help. You do a lot for yore ma." Daisy waited for him to look at her. "Yore a good boy and a fine worker all by yoreself. Remember that, Jamie."

" 'Es, Ma." Her son nodded happily as Daisy sloshed some water onto the floor and they began to scrub.

They giggled and made zigzags and circles as they cleaned. Jamie liked to help clean, and this was one of his favorite things about Miz Willow's house. He could help with the floors without anybody carrying him.

Daisy handed him a dry rag and took one herself. She dried a swath through the middle of the cabin, while Jamie scooched around to help mop up the water. After they finished, Daisy helped him get ready for bed. It'd been a long day.

As she wove her needle through the intricate mesh of the netting she used to create fine filet lace, Daisy fumed. She'd always tried to let Jamie think he could do things as well as anybody else.

"Wurk dun better. . . ." The words echoed in her mind and rankled. Bryce had no call to tell her son the work he did alone wasn't good enough. Come to think of it, he'd said something like that to her the other day — about asking for help. Well, she didn't need Bryce's help, and she didn't want Jamie thinking he did, either. She and her son worked hard, loved each other, and made it through each day grateful for what they had. It might not be much, and they might not do things the way everybody else did, but her son was just as good as any other boy in the holler. And she wouldn't allow Bryce to

let Jamie think otherwise.

When that Bryce Chance gets back, I'll have a little chat with him, Daisy decided. *We don't need him trying to change anything.*

"Yore fixin' to make a powerful change with this." The general store owner, Mr. Norton, thumped the big crate decisively.

"Yep," Bryce agreed, eyeing the crate with grave misgiving. It seemed a lot larger than he'd expected. Maybe they'd packed it in with a lot of stuff so it'd have safe shipping.

"Let's get 'er into yore wagon." Mr. Norton punctuated the order by narrowly missing the spittoon sitting outside the store. "Aw, now I'll hafta clean that."

Bryce doubted it. From the looks of that spittoon and the porch around it, Mr. Norton rarely cleaned it — but he missed often.

The enormous crate barely fit in the wagon, and even then, it took Bryce, Mr. Norton, and three other men who'd happened to see them struggling and lent a hand. Cast iron made for a heavy load.

"Thank you, gentlemen." Bryce slapped his hat back on his head before shaking their hands. He was set to go when he remembered something.

"Mr. Norton, would you mind bringin' out that mirror you already wrapped up?"

He wondered what Daisy would say when he showed it to her. It was tangible proof that he'd listened. He'd probably get one of those glowing smiles of hers that made him feel warm clear down to his toes. He jumped onto the buckboard and flicked the reins. It was time to get back home.

Good thing I started out early this morning, Bryce reflected. The horses were having a rough go of it. *I understand why — the thing's heavier'n an ox stuck in a mudhole.*

He pulled the wagon over to the side of the road when he heard the unmistakable gurgle of a mountain stream. He unhitched the team and led them to the water, letting them drink their fill and cool off.

"There you go, girls. You've worked hard today, and we've still got a ways to go." Bryce spoke softly, patting the faithful mares' necks one after another. "I'll give you some sugar lumps later, after your rubdown. But first we've got to get back. Ready?"

Both horses nosed his palm one last time with velvety muzzles before giving soft whickers and turning around.

"Good girls." Bryce let them know how much he appreciated their hard work. Too many people expected animals to push, pull, and carry things for them without so much as a thank you. Some didn't even give them enough rest or food, either. Bryce shook his head at the thought. How could anyone look into the eyes of a horse and not know it deserved to be cared for in return for its loyalty and hard work? To Bryce's way of thinking, treating animals right just made good sense.

Refreshed by the break, the horses managed to trot a bit faster despite their heavy burden. Bryce came to the fork in the road just as the sun began to set. A few hundred yards farther, he pulled up to Miz Willow's barn.

Bryce's stomach rumbled loudly as he unhitched the team. The horses deserved to be taken care of first — after all, they'd worked a lot harder today than he had! He'd just led them to their stalls when Daisy walked into the barn.

"Hello, Daisy." It was good to see her in her pretty blue dress. But something wasn't right. He noticed it in her gait — if she'd been a horse, he'd've figured she'd gotten a rock wedged in her shoe.

CHAPTER 6

Daisy walked toward Bryce stiffly, her arms crossed in front of her and her jaw set. To be sure, something had caused a hitch in her getalong.

"Bryce." Daisy didn't say another word until she stood in front of him.

He waited. No sense trying to find shelter until you knew which way the wind blew.

"We need to talk."

Uh-oh. Men never said that. Women did — and only when they were angry. Bryce knew from living on Chance Ranch with four sisters-in-law that if a woman said "We need to talk" it roughly translated to: "If I were a man, I'd've given you a shiner, but I'm more civilized than that, so I have to get the message across another way."

"All right." Bryce fought the urge to cross his own arms. The last thing he wanted to do was intimidate her. Whatever was on her mind, it was important to her, and that meant he needed to hear it.

"I know you're trying to be a friend to Jamie, and I appreciate it," she began.

There was a "but" lurking in there somewhere. Bryce waited it out.

"But . . ."

There it is. I knew it!

"I don't think I've been clear about the way I choose to raise my son." She paused to look at him expectantly.

He had no idea what she expected. Somewhere along the line, he'd managed to botch things up, but he hadn't a clue where. An uncomfortable silence filled the barn before Daisy let out an exasperated breath.

"I've tried my best to raise my son with the knowledge that he's as good as everybody else." She glared up at him, challenging him to disagree with her.

The lioness was protecting her cub. Daisy's eyes lit with an amber fire, glowing through in her indignation.

"He is just as good as everybody else," Bryce agreed readily. "Better than most, I'd say."

She visibly deflated. He'd stolen the wind from her sails. The anger left her eyes, leaving behind two empty pools of hurt. Bryce ached to hold her close. He'd caused her

61

pain somehow, and he wanted to make it right.

"Then why did you tell Jamie he couldn't do things well enough by himself?"

"I never said that." Bryce felt as though he'd been punched in the gut.

"Yes, you did!" She blazed with anger once again. "You told him the work was done better if he did it with someone else!"

"Something's not right here. True, I tried to teach Jamie that working with someone isn't any cause for shame." The boy's ma already had an aversion to asking for help, but Bryce wanted Jamie to know it was all right.

"Work together is done better," Daisy chanted.

"Oh." Bryce finally understood. "Close, but not quite. I taught him that work is better when done together — it's more fun being part of a team. It makes the time go faster." A sudden thought chilled him to the bones. "I was so sure Jamie understood what I meant. Does he think I was saying he wasn't good enough?"

"No." Daisy practically shrank before his eyes. "I thought that's what you meant. Jamie said he and I were a good team when we swept the floor, and then he repeated that rhyme. . . . He swapped the words a little, but I'm the one who messed up the meaning." She bit her lip. "I'm so sorry, Bryce. I could hardly believe that you would think that, but my son . . ." Her voice trailed off.

"Is your priority." Bryce finished the sentence for her. "I understand you were protecting your own, Daisy. It was just a mix-up."

"Thanks, Bryce." She managed a tight smile. "I don't know how to make it up to you."

"I do." Bryce grinned. "What's for supper?"

How could I have been so foolish? Bryce Chance never gives anything to me and mine save kindness, and I repay him with accusation and suspicion. Daisy paced the floor as Miz Willow and Jamie slept, berating herself.

Do I trust him when he's never given me a reason not to? No, I jump to conclusions. Then do I ask him about it? Give him a chance to explain? No. I barge into his barn like a mother hen with my feathers ruffled, ready to peck him to death with my angry words. And after I've accused him of faults he doesn't possess, he understands. He forgives me and acts like I never spoke a rotten word to him.

He's a good and wise man, that Bryce

Chance. Jamie's lucky to learn from him for however long he stays. I'm glad he's here. I jist wish I could say the same thing about myself. When I think of how I treated him, I could sink into the dirt like a worm.

"Tomorrow I'll do better," she resolved as she finally crawled into bed.

The next morning, Daisy awoke feeling better than she had in two days. Bryce was back, and better still, he hadn't insulted Jamie and never would.

Daisy jumped out of bed and hurried to get dressed. She'd make a huge mess of flapjacks to celebrate. It was going to be a wonderful day.

Bryce tapped on the door while she set the platter of food on the table. Miz Willow slid the comb through Jamie's hair one last time.

"Come on in," she called.

"Morning." Bryce stood for a second in the doorway as he always did, probably letting his eyes adjust. After the bright morning sunshine, the cabin seemed dim in comparison.

His broad shoulders filled the doorway, the sun catching his brown hair and giving it a rich glow. His image alongside Daisy's recollection of his kindness the night before made him seem larger than life as he stepped inside.

"Hi, Byce!" Jamie scooched urgently across the floor and flung his arms in the air.

Bryce didn't hesitate a second to scoop the little boy into his arms. "Mornin', Jamie."

"Mor'in'," Jamie repeated excitedly.

"Do you remember what I told you I'd bring back when I left?" Bryce leaned close and spoke in a loud whisper. Daisy heard every word.

So he had told Jamie he'd have to be gone for a short time. Jamie wasn't sad when she told him; he was remembering that Bryce had shared a secret with him.

Jamie glanced around the cabin at Daisy and Miz Willow before putting a finger to his lips.

"Not anymore, buddy." Bryce turned Jamie a bit so they both faced the women. "Now we get to tell them. We're going to be hauling in a . . ." Bryce nodded at Jamie to finish telling the surprise.

"Sofe!" Jamie threw his hands up in the air.

"That's right. A stove." Bryce set Jamie down at the table and sat beside him. "And not just any old stove. This one's for heating and for cooking."

"Glory be!" Miz Willow beamed at them. "The Chance family bought Hattie and Logan a kitchen range stove! What a surprise for when they get back."

"Wonderful!" Daisy exclaimed. Cooking would be a lot simpler with a stove, once she and Hattie learned to use it. "We'll have to move a few things. . . ."

"No, it's far too big to fit in Hattie and Logan's room." Bryce beamed. "Besides, the cooking is done in here anyway. Just makes sense."

Daisy couldn't stop smiling at that. It did make sense, and it made sure that everyone was included. A stove would mean a warmer winter for Miz Willow's rheumatiz and less chance for stray sparks. She'd sleep better knowing her son wouldn't face another fire.

After breakfast — Daisy noticed with satisfaction how Bryce happily polished off the last few flapjacks — she and Bryce went to open up the crate. Miz Willow had taken Jamie to visit with a few young children in the area.

"Shore is big," Daisy observed.

"I thought the same thing," Bryce admitted. "I hope it has a lot of packing straw inside for shipping."

"We'll see." Daisy grabbed one of the hammers to start prying off some nails.

66

"Wait a minute." Bryce stopped her.

"You want to start on the other side?" She craned her neck to get a better view.

"No. I want to show you something." Bryce handed her a flat package.

"It's for Hattie and Logan, but it was your idea." His smile seemed a little shy. "Open it."

Daisy unwound the brown paper to uncover a framed mirror a little bigger than the one on Miz Willow's wall.

"You remembered!" She traced the wooden oval that was decorated with vines similar to those Otis Nye had carved on the wedding chest. "It matches the chest so well. Hattie will love it."

Bryce's grin filled her heart. He hadn't agreed that a mirror was strictly necessary, but he trusted her and was thoughtful enough to follow through. He surprised her at every turn.

"Let's go hang it above the washstand," he suggested.

She nodded, following him into the cabin. He pounded in a nail at the right height, and she reached up to hang it.

"Whoa." Bryce's hands covered hers as the frame slipped. The metal ring on the back of the frame hadn't caught on the nail.

He was so close, his arms reaching over

her shoulders, his hands warm and rough on hers. Heat coursed through her. She hadn't been this close to a man since Peter died, and she had forgotten how safe and cherished it made her feel.

Why would she remember that now, with a man she already knew would leave soon? Bryce Chance was a good man, but surely he didn't feel anything for the plump widow with a four-year-old son. When Jamie was born, she'd become a mother. Why did Bryce remind her she was still a woman?

Daisy felt so soft against him, fresh and sweet like some kind of flower after the rain. Her hair brushed softly against his sleeve; her hands seemed so small and smooth beneath his.

Her surprise was reflected in the mirror. Daisy's golden locks and fair skin glowed next to his dark hair and sun-darkened skin. Her pink mouth opened in an *O* of surprise; her brown eyes looked deep and dreamy.

She made him feel big and strong, powerful to protect her against the world, and all he wanted was to hold her safe. He didn't realize he'd been holding his breath until Daisy slipped her hands from beneath his and moved away.

He stood for a moment, bereft, before

sliding the mirror into place and clearing his throat. He stared into her eyes.

"Looks good to me." He didn't mean only the mirror, but Daisy didn't acknowledge what had passed between them.

"Jist right." She patted her hair. "Now let's go see about that stove." She led the way out the door, but Bryce didn't mind. Daisy was worth going after.

CHAPTER 7

Bryce hitched the horses to the wagon and had them pull the stove as close to the door as possible before tying the stove directly to the harness. It was the only way to get the box out of the wagon. Then he tackled trying to open it.

"There!" With a final heave of the crowbar, the front of the crate opened wide. Bryce stared at the stove, which took up almost the entire space inside the crate.

Whoever boxed it hadn't used a lot of packing straw; they hadn't needed to. The crate itself made a tight fit, with little chance the stove would slide around and become damaged.

"It's incredible!" Daisy walked around it, looking from every angle. "A wood-burning stove, a kitchen range top, and even an oven built right in!" She opened the oven door experimentally and peeked inside.

Bryce smiled at her excitement. The stove

was a beauty all right, but he didn't see how he could move it. If it had come in pieces or could be disassembled, he'd have managed. As it was, the thing was fully constructed with the pieces welded together. It had already been difficult to ease it out of the wagon onto a haystack and down to the ground. Bryce didn't see how he could move it to the cabin.

"I'll go get the pie tins." Daisy rushed off before Bryce could ask her what she was talking about. She returned in a moment with four metal pie tins.

"Ready?" she asked expectantly, crouching beside one of the stove feet.

"For what?" Bryce hated to admit it, but he had no idea what she was doing.

"You lift up the edge, and I'll slide the pie tin under the leg. We do it four times; then we can slide the stove to the door." She blinked at him. "It's too heavy to lift."

"Right." Bryce hefted one corner of the stove. Pie tins weren't wheels. He had his doubts about this scheme.

Once the pie tins were in place, Daisy hopped around, pushing aside bits of wood to clear a path. When she gave the signal, Bryce got behind the stove and gave it a mighty heave, expecting the heavy thing to scarcely budge.

He just about ended up on the ground for his doubts as the thing slid a goodly distance.

"It works!" He couldn't hide his amazement. The metal pie tins made the stove slide smoothly across the hard-packed dirt. He'd never have thought of this in a million years.

"Of course it does," Daisy teased him with an amused grin. "So how about putting those pie tins to work?"

"Yes, ma'am." Bryce put his hands on the stove and slid it to the doorstep.

"We'll have to lift this monster to get it inside on the wooden floor," he mused. "I'll go in backwards and lift while you push it on the two back feet. It'll slide forward, and then I'll yank it inside."

"Sounds good."

Bryce backed into position, stepping inside and crouching to lift the bottom of the stove the requisite few inches. "Now!"

He pulled, Daisy pushed, and a resounding *cra–a–ack* rent the air as the stove lodged itself in the doorframe. Bryce let go, but the stove didn't move. He put his hands on the range and leaned over it to get a view from the outside.

"It's splintered the doorway," Daisy moaned, hovering close. She squinted and stepped back. "Mayhap if I try and yank it back —"

"Nothing doing," Bryce stated firmly. "If the weight of the thing itself won't tilt it, there's precious little you or I can do. The thing's about two inches too wide to get inside the building."

"What're we gonna do?"

"Stand back, Daisy," Bryce ordered. "I'm going to have to try and push it back out."

"All right, Bryce. Go ahead."

He gave the stove a quick shove, but the thing didn't budge. He put his weight into it, digging in with his feet and using all the force he could muster.

"I'm out of the way now," Daisy clarified.

Bryce couldn't help it. After three days of miscommunication, hefting, and transporting the stove . . .

"It's stuck," he admitted.

"Stuck?" Daisy repeated dumbly. "Just how hard a push did I give that thing?" She walked up to the blocked doorway before venturing an opinion. "Mayhap if I wiggle it a little . . ." She grasped the edges and tried to move it from side to side, hoping to loosen the metal from where it jammed in the wooden doorframe.

She leaned back as Bryce leapfrogged over

the stove and slid down the flat range to stand beside her. Together they looked at the very heavy problem.

"So . . . no new stove inside the cabin." Daisy spoke more to break the silence than to really contribute. This had her stumped.

"And no doorway at all," Bryce finished woefully.

"Miz Willow and Jamie will be back in a couple hours," Daisy fretted. "What are we going to do?"

"If we can't get the stove in," Bryce said, "we'll have to get the doorframe out. If you go to the far left corner of the barn, you'll find the toolbox. Bring that and an ax from the wall. I'll get back inside and start taking the door off its hinges to give us more work space."

Daisy watched as he carefully squeezed through the doorway, somehow managing not to bang his head on his way through. Then she hurried to the barn, found the tools, and brought them back.

Bryce had already popped the door off its hinges and leaned it against the far wall. She passed him the saw. He squinted at the frame and placed the saw a few inches above where the stove stuck out.

Daisy stepped back. The doorframe was made of three pieces; the two long ones connected by the short one at the top.

"Wait a minute! Why don't you try separating the door-jamb at the top? It's gonna be awful hard to saw hunks out of that frame."

"Hmm." Bryce stepped back and craned his neck upwards. "I see what you mean." He pulled over one of the benches. "Would you give me a hammer?"

She passed him one and watched as he pried loose the nails joining the wood together, then worked the top beam free. He clasped his hands around one of the sides and tugged.

Cre–e–eak. The wood protested ominously as Bryce tried to angle it a little. He hopped down from the bench.

"Easiest thing to do will be using a chisel to split the board longways, then pull it apart."

"All right." Daisy rummaged for a chisel and rubber mallet.

"The stove being jammed in already started a crack." Bryce ran his hand along the frame. "I'll continue it."

He was as good as his word. After expanding the crack, he asked for the crowbar and pried the wood apart.

"I'll take care of it from this side, Bryce." Daisy wielded the crowbar with precious little skill but more than enough determination. Soon she'd torn the last of the doorframe from around the stove.

"I think," Daisy panted, tossing the last fragment away, "this should be the first wood we burn."

Bryce's laughter rumbled over her, the deep sound sweeping away her frustration and making her see the humor in the situation. She started to laugh, too.

After they recovered, they managed to coax and shove the stove into the cabin. Daisy gathered the pie tins, and they pushed the cast-iron monster into place.

"Ah," Bryce drew out the appreciative sound, "the time and effort saved by modern technology."

Daisy was giggling again. They stood side by side, each with more splinters than they could count, surveying the ruined doorway.

"I won't be able to rebuild it tonight," Bryce assessed. "You, Jamie, and Miz Willow will have to sleep in Hattie and Logan's room tonight."

"Fine by me." Daisy stretched her aching arms. "Doesn't matter where I am. I'm shore I'll sleep jist fine."

CHAPTER 8

The next morning, after a quick breakfast of day-old bread and butter with milk, they all headed to the school building for church.

"Beautiful mornin'," Daisy remarked, toting Jamie on her hip.

"Yep." Bryce, his stride shortened so he wouldn't outpace her and Miz Willow, took in a deep, appreciative breath of the fresh mountain air. He held out his arms to take Jamie, giving her a much-needed rest.

"We cain fix the door tomorra. I aim to enjoy the day." Daisy hoped Bryce felt the same way. He might be used to hauling heavy loads — his broad shoulders and strong arms certainly attested to that — but she wasn't. That stove had been far too heavy, and she, for one, was glad to have a day of rest before tackling the broken door-frame.

"Right."

"Good thing we're goin' to the Lindens'

for Sunday dinner." Miz Willow chuckled. "I don't know what I would've done iff'n Otis Nye, Rooster, and Nessie were expectin' to come to our place. No door to open for 'em, stove ain't ready to cook on, and it blocks my hearth! It'd be a fine sight to see me and Daisy rushin' around like that."

"True." Daisy gave a small laugh, but the rueful look on Bryce's face stopped her. "It's been a lot of work, but that's a mighty fine gift. I reckon having such a grand stove'll be more'n worth the wait. Bryce's been so clever in figgurin' out how to get the thang inside, the rest should jist fly by. Ev'rythang'll be up and runnin' afore Hattie and Logan get back."

Bryce's shoulders relaxed, and though he didn't smile outright, Daisy knew he understood her appreciation. He'd worked hard and deserved for it to be acknowledged.

In a few minutes they slid onto their bench and bowed their heads while Asa Pleasant, filling in for the circuit preacher, prayed.

"Lord, we ask to feel Your presence in this place as we gather together to worship You and strengthen our knowledge of all You are. Please bless this congregation and let it be a fruitful time. Amen."

Lord, please give me the strength I need to

take care of Jamie. I have a lot of work ahead of me to provide for my son. Let me have the will and the determination to see it through. Holp me to figgur out what I need to do. Amen.

Daisy rose to her feet, cradling Jamie on her hip, as they began to sing the hymns. *Funny how I cain't hear Bryce's voice so much as feel it next to me. Like a cat purring. I know it's there, happy and reassuring, but it ain't like Asa's raspy voice up there.*

As they began a favorite folk song, Bryce's comforting rumble stopped. Daisy could tell he was listening hard, trying to catch the words:

"Enoch lived to be three hundred and sixty-
    five,
And then the Lord came down and took
    him up to heaven alive. . . ."

They moved through the other verses about Paul being freed from prison, Moses and the burning bush, Adam and Eve, each time coming back to the chorus:

"I saw, I saw the light from heaven
Come shinin' all around.
I saw the light come shining.
I saw the light come down."

By the third time they sang the refrain,

Bryce joined in with them. Daisy smiled as the praise rolled out of him so low and deep it flowed under all the other voices. *His sangin' fits him — quiet and not showy but powerful strong.*

The next morning, Miz Willow took Jamie out to the garden for an outdoor lesson. Daisy had taken care of the herb garden, but the vegetable garden needed weeding.

Bryce brought out a yardstick and wrote down the dimensions for the doorframe. Then he and Daisy checked out the lumber left over from building Logan and Hattie's new home. After selecting three pieces of the right width, she and Bryce worked at sawing them to be the proper length. Bryce finished the first two before coming over and polishing off the one she hadn't gotten through.

"I don't know how you do it," Daisy marveled aloud. Bryce's shoulders rippled beneath his tan cambric shirt as he worked the saw.

"Practice," Bryce answered as he finished. "Lots and lots of it."

Next they needed to sand the wood smooth. Bryce handed her a piece of sandpaper, and they got to work.

Daisy took the rough paper and scrubbed

at the lumber vigorously. She had enough splinters to last through the rest of the year.

"Easy." Bryce came up alongside her. He reached over and put his hand atop hers, leaning in and pulling back. "You don't have to attack it. Simple, straight strokes."

Daisy's arm tingled. She turned her head the slightest bit and barely refrained from burying her face in his chest. Bryce smelled so good, like sawdust and leather and strong soap.

He let go, and Daisy had to force herself to keep sanding. Suddenly, the afternoon felt cold. She hoped this project would be finished soon — she didn't know how much longer she could work alongside him and not push back that errant lock of wavy brown hair that teased his strong brow.

As Bryce continued working, he noticed how rough the sandpaper was. He'd used it often in his life but never realized how coarse the paper felt beneath his fingertips. Daisy's hand had been so soft — had she noticed how rough his own palm was?

He shook away the pesky thoughts. He'd never met a woman any finer than Daisy Thales. She didn't demand he entertain her or even expect him to try to fill the air with meaningless chitchat. Daisy made him feel comfortable — except for when being near her made him ache to hold her closer.

And he couldn't. Strong though his attraction to her had grown, Bryce had noticed how Daisy made it more than clear she didn't need him. She'd already lost the man she loved, worked hard to build a life for herself and her son, and was trying to regain what the fire took from them. Daisy had made her plans, and he wasn't a part of them. When he left, it would be easier to quell his urge to take her in his arms, but now, while she filled the house and his mind, he struggled.

Lord, I know this is not the woman for me. She isn't interested in me and has no place for a new husband in her plans, much less one who would take her and her son from everything and everyone they love. My home is Chance Ranch, my place beside my family. Daisy works so hard to make a life for her and Jamie here. They've lost so much. I can't pursue her with the aim of making them leave behind the few things they have. I won't try to make her feel for me what I feel for her. Lord, please take away my longing and let me enjoy her and Jamie's friendship instead. Amen.

After a quick break for a hasty lunch of bread, cheese, and apples — with the stove not hooked up and still blocking the hearth, no cooking could be done — he and Daisy finished reconstructing the doorframe.

Daisy shut the door, then opened it again before passing judgment. "Perfect!"

"Snug, but it shouldn't stick." Bryce nodded. It would hold out drafts and danger, keeping Miz Willow — and Daisy and Jamie — warm and safe.

"I'll have the stove installed tomorrow morning," Bryce planned aloud. "We'll need to move it over near the table for tonight so it doesn't block the heat or the beds. Where are those pie tins?"

"Jist a minute." Daisy rummaged around on the shelves and pulled them down. After they'd slid the stove to the foot of the bed, she put her hands on her hips. "Seems to me I better get some supper going."

"I'm not going to argue with that." Bryce laughed. They'd worked hard for two days. A hearty meal would go a long way to renew his strength.

He left her bustling around the hearth and went to clear up the area where they'd prepared the lumber. He threw the scraps on the woodpile, which would need attention. He and Logan hadn't cut nearly enough to last the cabin through a long mountain winter, and that was before they'd put on the addition, which would need heat through the cold months, as well.

He gathered the sawdust and added it to the barrelful he and Logan had collected already. Sawdust was good for the stables — coated the floor and helped with the barn smell.

As he worked, the crisp crunch of fallen leaves beneath his boots caught his attention. Autumn, bringing with it bold colors of gold and red, had touched the holler. Soon the fall shades would take the place of all the green of summer. Bryce had to leave before winter; his time here was growing short.

Which meant he had to make the most of it. He fetched a rake from the barn and attacked the leaves, drawing them into a single pile.

Not big enough. Bryce had already cleared the way from the barn to the cabin, but the pile didn't yet suit his purpose. He went around the barn and on the other side of Hattie and Logan's room to gather more leaves. He corralled them into one huge pile — big as a small haystack — in the middle of the cleared area.

"Can I borrow Jamie here for a minute?" Bryce stuck his head through the doorway. "I need his opinion on something."

Jamie looked at his mama with the big

brown eyes so like hers. Bryce saw Daisy hesitate, then smile.

"Of course." She gave her permission without asking Bryce what he wanted to do.

Good. She was learning to trust him. She needed to loosen the apron strings a little so Jamie could try more things.

"Why don't you come with us?" Bryce scooped the little boy into his arms and tromped back outside. He knew Daisy followed.

He stopped just outside the door and made a show of surveying the land. Jamie's big eyes looked around eagerly.

"Nope. Guess I must've left it a little farther away." Bryce turned past the side of the cabin and stopped again. He smiled as Jamie peered around excitedly. Daisy cast a quick look around, then, seeing nothing, sent Bryce a questioning glance.

"Hmm . . . I know I left it around here somewhere." Bryce made a show of looking around before turning the corner once again and letting out a triumphant "Ha!" He bounced Jamie a bit. "Now isn't that the biggest pile of leaves you ever saw in your life?" Bryce waited for the little boy's nod.

"Do you know what we do with leaf piles?" Jamie shook his head.

"Well, I'd better show you!" Bryce held

Jamie aloft. "Ready?"

Jamie barely nodded when Bryce tossed him high in the air, sending the shrieking boy toppling into the massive pile of leaves.

CHAPTER 9

"Jamie!" Daisy screamed as she ran to the pile of leaves. What if he'd hit his head or broken an arm? Her baby lay shrieking in fear and probably pain, or —

Laughter! Jamie rolled around in the huge pile, flailing his arms and twisting around to make the leaves crunch. As she knelt beside him in the pile — even under their weight, neither touched the hard ground — her son gathered handfuls of leaves and threw them up to shower around them.

"F–un!" Jamie giggled when he got back enough of his breath. He struggled to sit up on the shifting pile, then gave a few experimental bounces.

"Oh," Daisy gasped and gathered him close. Praise the Lord he wasn't hurt. She'd heard that piercing shriek and thought the worst.

"Go." Jamie wriggled out of her grasp and flopped back in the leaves.

Daisy drew a deep breath and stood up. She turned around to find Bryce regarding her with those deep blue eyes of his. She smoothed back her hair and walked up to him.

"You gave me a fright, Bryce Chance," she said, admitting what he already must know.

"I'd never hurt Jamie," he responded in a low voice, so the little boy wouldn't hear.

"I know," Daisy apologized in those two words. "I heard him shrieking like that, and I was afeared. . . ." Her voice trailed off as they both watched her son happily crunching leaves. "I've never heard him laugh like that."

Jamie smiled almost all the time, always ready with a giggle to lift her heart. But this spontaneous cry of joy, the adventurous yell of a little boy exploring the world, was new. For both of them.

She looked around. It was early in the season to have raked up so much foliage. Bryce had purposely gone all around the barn and house to make a pile big enough so Jamie would be safe. He'd thought up a way to give Jamie a new experience and make the little boy feel daring without danger. She'd never have thought of something like this.

"Thankee, Bryce." She remembered his apparent discomfort when thanked, only after the words were spoken. *I hope I didn't embarrass him again.*

"You're welcome." Bryce grinned at her, his easy acknowledgment warming her heart.

"Ag'n?" Jamie's eager question caught their attention.

"I don't know." Daisy surveyed the flattened and scattered pile doubtfully.

"Hold on, buddy." Bryce hauled Jamie out of the pile and deposited him in Daisy's arms. He grabbed the rake he'd probably used in the first place and busily set about reconstructing the pile. He reached for Jamie, and Daisy willingly gave him up.

"Wait." Bryce sat Jamie down where he could lean up against the wall. "I think something's missing."

Too late, Daisy realized what Bryce intended as he headed her way. She let out a flustered "Eek!" as his strong hands closed around her waist. She didn't have time to enjoy the sensation before she went sailing through the air and crunching through the leaves.

"Bryce Chance!" she blustered, struggling to extricate herself.

"Yes?" He stood over her, holding Jamie.

"This was supposed to be for Jamie." She tried to scowl but couldn't manage it in the face of her baby's delighted smile.

"You're right." Bryce jumped in beside her, sending Jamie crashing though the leaves and into her arms.

She laughed so hard her sides hurt, and Jamie giggled right along. Finally, she was able to stand up and move Jamie to the edge of the pile. She needed to go check on dinner. She was about to tell Bryce as much when he started climbing out of the flattened mess, but then she changed her mind.

"Your turn." She planted her hands on Bryce's broad shoulders and shoved until he toppled back.

Jamie's laughter rent the air once more as he scooched over and pushed more leaves on top of Bryce. Daisy couldn't remember the last time they'd had so much fun.

"Whew," Bryce breathed as he leaned back and stretched. "I'm so full I couldn't eat another bite."

"I should hope not!" Daisy smiled to soften the words.

"Nothin' left even if yore stomach could hold it." Miz Willow looked at the empty dishes on the table.

The healer has a point, Daisy reflected.

Bryce alone had packed away three biscuits slathered with butter, two bowls of stew, and almost half of her fresh-baked apple pie.

She watched as he gave his stomach a satisfied pat, only to have a wince crease his face.

"Too full, Bryce?" She knew he was startled by the look he gave her.

"Nah. Can't get enough of your fine cooking, ladies." Bryce held up his left hand. "Stubborn splinter." He massaged the area around the wound.

"Why didn't you say so?" Miz Willow straightened up and came back with tweezers and some witch hazel. She filled a bowl with warm water. "Put yore hand in that for a mite, and the wood'll swoll up so it cain be picked out. Daisy'll hafta do it." The old woman looked ruefully at her hands, so gnarled with years of work and late rheumatism.

Daisy cleared the table as Bryce obediently stuck his hand in the bowl. It didn't fit, so he stuck his palm into the water with his fingers rising up out of the bowl.

I hope I cain get it without hurtin' him, Daisy fretted. *I should, after all the time I done spent doin' fine needlework.*

The memory of his hands on her as he

caught the mirror and later taught her to use sandpaper sent a shiver down her spine. Keeping steady while she felt the strength in his work-roughened palms would be far more difficult than embroidering lace.

After Miz Willow declared he'd soaked long enough, Daisy patted the area dry and looked at the splinter. The offending piece of wood, now plumped with water, made a dark, jagged path down Bryce's palm near his thumb. She slid her right hand beneath to hold it steady in the light before gingerly grabbing the edge of the wood with the tweezers. She held her breath as she tugged the splinter, having to work it to the sides a bit before it slid out. Blood filled the line made by the splinter as she cleansed the wound with witch hazel.

He didn't flinch or make a sound, even though it had been the biggest splinter Daisy had ever laid eyes on. *Must've hurt somethin' awful.*

He could hardly feel it. The second Daisy touched his hand, the pain lessened. When the trickle of blood stopped, Daisy released him.

"You're left-handed," Bryce spoke the realization aloud. She'd held his injured hand in her right and used the left to work the tweezers. How had he not noticed it before? Little wonder she'd had so much trouble with the saw — he'd had Daisy using her right hand.

"Yes. Always have been." Daisy gave the witch hazel back to Miz Willow.

"I never noticed before — I would've given you a different saw. Why didn't you tell me?"

"Didn't think it was important." She visibly bristled. "I don't need any extry help."

This is the way she lives her whole life. Not speaking up when she needs help, not trusting anyone else to care for her or her son properly. Does she even realize how thoroughly she cuts herself off from other people? She goes to church and teaches her son Bible verses, but Daisy relies only on herself. Who am I to point out her flaws when I'm not staying around anyway? Lord, she's been hurt and survived a lot of loss, but she still needs to lean on You.

It took the better part of the next day to get the stove set up and functioning properly. Bryce could hardly make heads or tails of the blurry, smudged instructions, so he ended up learning by trial and error.

Finally, Bryce stood back and surveyed his work. They'd put it in the original hearth cavity, but not all the way. The range and oven poked out for easy use. All in all, it hardly took up any more room than the original hearth, and it would work a lot better.

"Nice," Daisy said appreciatively.

"I hope so." Bryce scowled at the troublesome machine. "Two days to fetch and haul it back, one to destroy the doorway and get it inside. Another to repair the damage, and one more to set the contraption up. Five days of work." Bryce shook his head. "I was beginning to think it wouldn't be ready before Logan and Hattie got back!"

Daisy burst out laughing. The hearty, happy sound made Bryce smile in and of itself, but . . .

"What's so funny?"

"Oh!" Daisy gasped and pointed to the stove. "I was jist thinkin' now might not be the best time to point out how we left two pie tins under the back legs."

"No!" Bryce hunkered down and peered at the floor of the hearth. Sure enough, two pie tins lay beneath the stove legs, halfway into the recess of the hearth.

"I already put together the stovepipe and connected it to the flue." Bryce hung his head in frustration. "I can't lift it now."

"Cain't lift what now?" Miz Willow stood

in the cabin doorway.

"The stove, Miz Willow." Daisy gestured to the far wall. "We left two pie tins under the back feet."

"Hunh." Miz Willow squinted at her shelves for a minute. "Well, I had three, and Hattie brung a pair when she moved in, so I reckon we don't need 'em."

"Praise be." Bryce stood up and brushed stove black off his hands. "It's done then."

"Good thing, too." Miz Willow turned back outside to resume her lesson with Jamie. "Logan and Hattie'll be back tomorra."

CHAPTER 10

Daisy didn't see Hattie or Logan until the next night. But when the newly married couple arrived, they were tired and decided to go straight to bed. Daisy and Bryce met them in the barn to help unload the wagon and settle in the horses.

"It's late, and we ate some jerky and biscuits on the ride here," Logan explained.

"It's good to be home." Hattie yawned, but despite being tuckered out, she glowed from the time spent with her new husband.

Daisy felt a surge of gratitude toward Logan Chance for seeing beyond her sister-in-law's barrenness to the worth of the woman herself. He'd made Hattie happier than Daisy had seen her since before Horace Thales passed on.

Now that Hattie's remarried, she's not a Thales anymore, Daisy realized. *I wonder if that means we aren't sisters-in-law no more. Not that it matters. Hattie will always be kin in my heart.*

"Daisy and I'll help you carry in your bags," Bryce offered, winking at Daisy.

Ignoring the flutter caused by that wink, Daisy nodded and gathered up the luggage and purchases the newlyweds had brought home.

When they got to the cabin, Bryce opened the door but hung back near Daisy to let the happy couple inside first. They wearily headed straight to their room, completely missing the fact that the new stove now dominated the hearth. Daisy and Bryce exchanged a shocked look. He held a finger up to his lips, and she nodded. It could wait.

The glow from the small fire Daisy had set in the hearth in the newlyweds' room bathed the finished place.

"Look, Logan!" Hattie turned around to take everything in, still holding a saddlebag clutched to her chest. "The quilt is on the bed, and they moved the carved trunk." She dropped the saddlebags onto Logan's desk and walked over to the washstand. "Daisy, you hung the curtains and our new towels! What's this?" Hattie traced the carving around the mirror. "It's beautiful!" She enveloped her friend in a warm hug.

"We thought it'd be a nice surprise." Daisy hugged her back.

"You put up the mantel." Logan ran his hands across it. "And hung the pegs." He turned to beam at Bryce and Daisy. "You two finished everything!"

"Not everything." Bryce shrugged off the praise, but Daisy could tell he was pleased with their reaction.

"We put things in order," Daisy agreed, "but it takes love to make a house a home."

"With Hattie by my side and good friends around us" — Logan put an arm around his wife and smiled at everyone — "I think we've got a good start."

The next morning, Hattie made her way into the cabin's main room to help prepare breakfast. After hugging Miz Willow and swooping down on Jamie for a quick kiss on the forehead, she turned to the hearth.

"Is that a . . ." Hattie couldn't find the words, her blue eyes wide as saucers as she approached the new stove.

Daisy watched in silence as Hattie looked it over from top to bottom, holding out her hands to capture the fire's warmth. She waited until Hattie opened the oven door and sent the smell of rising cinnamon rolls swirling through the cabin.

"The Chances had it shipped to Kentucky from clear across the country," Daisy explained. "Bryce fetched it and hauled it back here while you were gone."

"It's wonderful," Hattie breathed, her eyes shining. "It looks complicated, though. I hope it wasn't too much trouble."

Daisy couldn't hold back the laughter that welled up at Hattie's innocent statement.

"What's got you laughing so hard, Daisy?" Logan asked as he and Bryce came inside.

Daisy couldn't catch her breath enough to repeat Hattie's words.

"I don't know." Hattie shook her head in confusion. "I just told her I hoped they didn't have to go to too much trouble to bring in the new stove."

Daisy almost had the spurts of laughter under control when Bryce's deep chuckles made her lose her composure again. They were the only ones who knew just how funny it was.

"I don't get it." Logan shrugged and walked over to inspect the stove. "Hey, are those pie tins under there?"

Daisy and Bryce just shook their heads and laughed harder as Miz Willow took over.

"What of it? I cain't think of a better place for a pie tin than the hearth!"

"How was yore honeymoon, Hattie?" Daisy asked after the men had finished breakfast and gone off to do chores. She shifted Jamie to her other hip. He was getting big.

"Wonderful!" Hattie's one-word answer said it all. Logan treated her right, and she was happy with the life she'd chosen.

"Good." Daisy stopped as Hattie stooped to harvest some leaves for her medicine satchel. "Meet anyone interestin'?"

"Yes. Jack Tarhill is a real sharp businessman with a good eye for detail." Hattie stopped talking and looked Daisy in the eye. "He noticed the new lace collar on my green dress and asked where I'd purchased it."

"That's nice." Daisy enjoyed hearing that such an astute man would remark on the quality of her work.

"Daisy, I know you've been doing business with Mitch Flaggart for years, but Jack asked me to try and change yore mind." Hattie waited for a response.

"I've relied on Mitch since I was jist a girl and Mama traded her lace with him." The lessons on making lace were some of Daisy's fondest memories of her mother. She loved it when the two of them sat quietly, needles moving rhythmically as they created something beautiful.

"Yep. But he's getting on in years, Daisy." Hattie paused, and Daisy nodded to acknowledge it was harder for Mitch to make the trip to Hawk's Fall — and would be harder still to get to Salt Lick. "And the fact of the matter is, Jack reckons he cain get a fine price for yore work."

The figure Hattie quoted stopped Daisy in her tracks. *So much money. I cain't cipher, but even I cain tell the difference is impressive. I hate to leave Mitch in the lurch, but I have to do what's best for Jamie and me.*

"He knows I work collars and veils and table runners — not christening gowns or hoods?" Daisy had to make sure the market was right. *Filet Lacis,* while stunningly intricate, wasn't pliable enough to use for those things. Tatted lace worked well, but Daisy didn't know that method.

"I tole him as much," Hattie affirmed. "He says it's hard to find yore fancy hand-made lace here in the States. Iff'n yore agreeable, he won't have to pay such hefty trading taxes, so you'll both come off well."

"That's good." Daisy nodded as much to herself as to Hattie and absentmindedly stroked Jamie's hair.

"He said summat about how yore lace is different than even the stuff he ships over. Summat about it going the other way?" Hattie puzzled aloud.

"I do it backward on account of bein' left-handed." Daisy smiled. She'd practiced enough with Mama to do it with her right, but she worked so much faster using her left.

"He says as how that makes it more rare." Hattie smiled.

"I suppose it might be so, but plenty of other thangs are more precious," Daisy said. "Thangs like family and friends."

"What've you decided to do about your share of Chance Ranch?" Bryce asked Logan as they mucked out the stalls later that morning. Each of the six brothers held equal stake, and Logan was owed his due even though he didn't plan to return.

"I telegraphed with Gideon and Paul while I was in Louisville," Logan admitted. "We're thinking the best thing to do is buy me out. I'll take a few of the horses and a few head of cattle. Whatever my share of land and other livestock amounts to, I'll take half the money value of what I'd get after taxes if we were selling it all outright."

"Only half?" Bryce echoed. "You're entitled to all of your portion, Logan."

"I know, but I'm not going to be around to work it. Besides, I'm the youngest, so we all know there was some time when I didn't pull enough weight for the equal split."

Logan grinned happily. "Truth is, I've got the business started up right here, and Hattie and I won't hurt for money. We have land, friends, steady income, and purpose. She's the healer, keeps the bodies around here hale and hearty. I negotiate trades and keep their finances healthy. That's more'n enough for any man."

"I understand." Bryce thought of all the new Chance children. The next generation would be much bigger than the six brothers who started out at Chance Ranch. They'd decided long ago that, regardless of how many children each brother had, the land would be redivided equally among their progeny when the time came ripe. Every Chance son and daughter would hold equal stake once more. Logan wouldn't have any children, so it made sense to let his brothers buy him out.

"I can't believe I'll be going back without you." Bryce spoke gruffly, slapping his brother on the shoulder. "Things just won't be the same."

"When things stay the same," Logan mused, "it means you're not growing. I hope Chance Ranch keeps on growing. I know I can depend on you to take care of things."

When did my baby brother become so seri-

ous and grown-up? He's a man now with a wife and a business. Logan's found his place and his purpose. I always figured mine was Chance Ranch, but I thought the same for Logan and was wrong.

Bryce saw Daisy walking with Hattie across the yard. *Seeing Daisy tugs something in me, especially when I think of leaving and never seeing her or Jamie again. Could those be growing pains?*

"Pretty, isn't she?" Logan had followed his gaze.

"Absolutely," Bryce agreed so fervently that Logan looked at him askance.

"She is my wife, Bryce." A steely glint lit Logan's eye as he planted his feet a bit wider.

"And I'm happy for you." Bryce tried to calm Logan down. "But there's nothing more beautiful than seeing women playing with a child."

Logan looked again toward the women, where Daisy held a squirming Jamie as Hattie tickled him. "It's a fine sight." Logan relaxed as he said the words. "But all the same, I'm happy to have Hattie all to myself."

"So I noticed," Bryce teased his brother with a grin. *But I can't imagine Daisy without Jamie. He brings out the loving mother, the strong lioness, the laughing girl, and the gentle homemaker in her. Jamie's a great kid, and he makes Daisy a better woman.*

"How much wood did you get cut while we were gone?" Logan's question snapped Bryce back to their conversation.

"About that . . ." Bryce launched into a shortened version of how the stove monopolized their week. "Between moving and setting up the stove and repairing the doorframe, I didn't get so much as a full cord cut."

"So that's why you and Daisy couldn't stop laughing this morning," Logan reasoned with a big grin. "I can't believe one little stove made you go through all that hassle."

"Little?" Bryce drew himself to his full height and jabbed a finger at his brother's chest. "Why don't you go try to haul that thing around?"

"Sorry!" Logan put his hands in the air. "It is pretty big."

"And heavy," Bryce added. "Thing's made of solid cast iron all welded together."

"Hmm. I wondered how it managed to survive all you put it through!" Logan laughed and slapped his hand on his knee. "Come on, let's go get to work. Aside from the wood chopping, I've been thinking we need to build a second barn. If I'm going to transport those horses and cattle here from Chance Ranch, Miz Willow's barn can't hold them, and they won't survive the winter."

"Right." Bryce frowned at the thought of any domesticated animal left out to contend with the snowy chill of an Appalachian winter. "Any other work you want to get out of me?"

"I don't know." Logan pretended to give the matter serious thought. "Cabin, chopped wood for winter, impossible stove installation, new barn. Nope. That's it, but I'll let you know if I think of anything else!"

CHAPTER 11

Thunk. Thunk. Clunk. Bryce grinned at Jamie's efforts. The night before, Bryce had cranked the hand-held drill to force peg-sized holes through a small piece of wood. He filled the holes with pegs, only a single whack apiece, so they stuck up and needed to be driven in. Today he'd balanced the board on two bricks, sat Jamie down in front of it with a small wooden mallet, and showed him what to do.

The little boy had been banging with plenty of enthusiasm — if precious little accuracy — ever since. Jamie liked being outside, doing "man" work with them. The mallet clattered from his little hands to the opposite side of the makeshift worktable. Bryce put down the ax he'd been using to chop firewood and loped over to put the tool back in Jamie's hands.

"Tanks, Byce." The little boy beamed at him before holding the mallet with both hands and pummeling the wooden peg. The exercise was good to increase his arm strength and improve coordination.

"You're welcome, buddy." Bryce looked down. "You've already finished two of them? Good job, Jamie!"

"Fun." Jamie waved the mallet exuberantly before losing hold of it again.

"Hold on there." Bryce took the small tool. "I'll be right back." He made his way to the barn and grabbed the drill. The mallet's handle was small, so it didn't take long to make a hole through the end. Bryce grabbed some twine and headed back to Jamie.

"Here." He knotted the twine through the new hole, then looped the other end around Jamie's wrist. "Now you'll be able to get it whenever it jumps out of your hands. Mallets are tricky that way."

"Yes." Jamie nodded seriously. He dropped the wooden hammer over the side of the board, then pulled it back using the twine. "Wurks!" He beamed and began thunking at the pegs again. After a few clumsy swipes, he managed to knock one of the pegs farther in.

"Looks like you've got things under control," Bryce told him. "I'll leave you to it."

" 'Kay."

■ ■ ■ ■

"Boys drank that water faster'n fish." Hattie wiped her hands on a tea towel. "Working up quite a thirst out there."

"I'll bet." Daisy looked up from kneading bread dough. "Jamie all right? I hope he ain't bothering 'em iff'n he gets bored."

"Happy as a raccoon with summat shiny." Hattie smiled. "Bryce drilled some holes and steadied in some pegs. Jamie's out there bangin' away with a tiny mallet."

"Oh?" Daisy hoped her son wouldn't come back from that little adventure with bruises dotting his hands. No, Bryce would watch over him. Jamie could have his fun and be fine. "That's nice." *I wonder how many times Bryce has had to pick up that mallet.*

"Works out well," Hattie said, answering Daisy's unspoken thought. "Bryce even drilled a hole in the mallet handle and tied some twine to it so Jamie can yank it back if it falls."

"That's clever of him. Right smart." Daisy dropped the dough back in a big bowl and covered it. "It's nice for Jamie to be out working with the men."

"Bryce doesn't say much, but he's a

thoughtful one." Hattie slanted Daisy a look she couldn't decipher.

"He says plenty without running his mouth," Daisy defended. "A body cain't always rely on words."

"I know. It's why he's so good with the animals — he has a kind heart that speaks for itself." Hattie smiled. "He's taken an interest in Jamie. Logan would never have thought to do something like that peg board."

"Maybe not." Daisy smiled. "Logan's too busy holpin' grown folks."

"He does have a heart for the people of the holler." Hattie's love shone through her voice. "Bryce tends to the animals and the children. I noticed it at the sang when they first got here — children like bein' 'round him."

"Jamie shore does. He ain't had a man around afore." Daisy drew a deep breath. "It'll be hard on him when Bryce goes back to Californy."

"Maybe." Hattie shrugged. "I know Logan'll miss his brother greatly, and I've grown fond of Bryce."

"He grows on you." Daisy thought of how Bryce had quietly undertaken to spend time with her son and come up with ways for him to do things she'd never thought possible. "I didn't take much notice of him before yore wedding, but then, suddenlike, he's become a big part of Jamie's life."

"Jist Jamie's?" Hattie raised her eyebrows.

"All of us." That was the closest Daisy dared come to admitting how much she'd miss Bryce for her own sake, not just Jamie's.

"Seems to me a man don't go out of his way and befriend a child without good reason." Hattie looked meaningfully at Daisy. "From what I hear, betwixt sprucing up our cabin and takin' care of this wonderful stove, you two stuck together whilst Logan and me were off on our honeymoon."

"I . . ." Daisy started to deny it but quickly shut her mouth. He'd done a lot for her that she'd never asked. On those occasions when his hands closed over hers, a bolt of heat shot straight down her spine.

Cain it be that I didn't misinterpret the look in his eyes? Could a man like Bryce Chance — tall, strong, capable, and able to have any woman he wanted — possibly be interested in me? Shorely not.

"I see." Hattie found her answer in Daisy's silence. "What about you, Daisy? Could you find room in yore heart and family for a man like Bryce?"

Yes. The answer came so swiftly it shocked

her. She closed her eyes to clear her thoughts. *But he's so different from Peter. How could I even think of caring for another man that way when the love of my life is gone forever?* Tears welled in her eyes.

"Don't talk nonsense, Hattie Thales — ahem, Hattie Chance." Daisy squared her shoulders and vigorously scrubbed the already-clean table. "Jist 'cause you have a happy second marriage, don't mean I'll get a chance."

"And here I was thinking that a certain Chance might be jist what you need." Hattie delivered that parting shot and sailed from the cabin.

"But yore wrong, Hattie," Daisy muttered even though no one was around to hear the words. "The last Chance is leavin' town. Soon."

"A barn raisin'? At this time of year?" Hattie gave voice to the questions Daisy wouldn't ask. "What for? We've already got one!"

"I know," Logan placated. "But I'm taking my share of the ranch in part cash, part livestock, sweetheart. The milk cow's getting on in years, and the mule's come up lame. I aim to bring in a few head of cattle and some horses, but we don't have enough room in the barn as yet. They'll be arriving on the train's cattle car in two weeks. I've already arranged for the conductor to stop at the bend before Hawk's Fall so we can pick 'em up."

"We can't leave them outside with winter comin' on," Bryce added.

"Yore right." Daisy threw in her two cents. "We'll spread the word. Folks oughtta be glad to come and lend a hand, what with all Logan and Hattie done for 'em." Logan had come to the holler and used his affability to get to know folks personally. He found out who could carve and who could trap fine pelts, then went to Louisville to arrange selling it all. Daisy's lace would be the most recent addition, so she knew from experience just how grateful they all had cause to be.

"Holler's full of good people," Logan agreed. "Bryce and I've arranged for the lumber to come two days from now. Thick beams enough to build onto the existing structure. Between now and then, Bryce and I'll be carving a door outta the far wall so it'll all end up being one big barn."

"Yep." Bryce rocked back on his heels. "Going to get the word out. We'll be raisin' it next Saturday, if all goes well."

"Logan Chance, that's only four days from now!" Hattie shook her head in disbelief. "We have to get ready! You better hitch up the wagon. Daisy and I need to go to town to buy supplies. There'll be a lot of mouths to feed come Saturday, even if people bring vittles with them."

"No problem." Logan made his way toward the door. "That's why we told you early in the morning. We oughtta have plenty of time for a nice ride to the mercantile."

"Oh, no you don't." Daisy caught Bryce's arm as he followed Logan. "Hattie and I'll go. You and Logan have a lot of work ahead of you."

"What do you mean?" Bryce asked.

"Believe it or not" — Hattie bit back a grin — "we're gonna need those pie tins."

"Pie tins," Logan grumbled as he squeezed beside the stove. He was thinner than Bryce, so he had to contort himself into the hearth. "What on earth possessed you to use pie tins?"

"Daisy's idea." Bryce handed him the tools so Logan could start disassembling the stovepipe.

"Where'd she get a cotton-headed notion like that?" Logan demanded, clanking around.

"I don't know, but I'm mighty glad she

did." Bryce jumped to Daisy's defense. "Just you wait until you try to move this thing. I never would've moved it more than a yard if it wasn't for her 'cotton-headed notion.' "

"All right, I didn't mean anything by it." Logan came as close to apologizing as anyone could expect. "But how'd you go and forget to take 'em off before you put it together?"

"Not sure." Bryce thought about how fast he'd worked to pull this whole thing off. He'd botched it so badly, he didn't want Daisy to think he was inept.

"Huh?" Logan craned his neck to stare at Bryce. "You must have been distracted by something."

"I don't know." Bryce wished his brother would quit staring at him and get back to work. "We tried so hard to get this thing together, it's not surprising we overlooked one tiny detail."

"We?" Logan kept right on staring.

"Daisy and me."

"Aahh." Logan raised his eyebrows. "Distracted by a woman. Makes sense to me."

"Hey, don't talk like that." Bryce started, surprised at his own anger. "Daisy wasn't in the way at all. I couldn't have gotten this thing up and running without her."

"I didn't mean she was in the way or

messed up, Bryce." Logan grinned at his brother. "Sounds to me like it wasn't her fault at all. Just how much time have you two been spending together?"

"Daisy's an honorable woman," Bryce thundered.

"I know." Logan held up his hands in surrender. "But seems to me you've taken quite an interest in her son." He paused for a moment, but there had never been a time when Logan didn't speak the full weight of what was on his mind. "I think you've taken a liking to Jamie's mama."

"We've become friends," Bryce hedged.

"Just friends?"

"She's a beautiful woman with a fine boy." Bryce wouldn't come any closer to admitting his attraction. "Daisy's worked hard to build a life for herself and her son. I have a lot of respect for her."

"I see."

Bryce waited for Logan to say something else, but for once, his chatty brother worked in silence.

What does he see? Bryce wondered. *Since when does he let a subject drop without having the last word? Well, whatever it is he thinks he sees, he's wrong. Daisy doesn't need me, and I've got a life back in California. Doesn't mean we can't be civil to each other while I'm here. Logan's just twisted things in his mind.*

"Ouch!" Logan's head banged against the hearth wall.

"Well, what do you know?" Bryce teased. "That was a pretty loud clunk. Must be somethin' in there, after all."

CHAPTER 12

"Pot roast?" Miz Willow sounded off.

"Warmin' in the oven," Daisy answered.

"Rabbit stew?" she demanded.

"Simmerin' on the range," Hattie responded.

"Mashed taters? Carrots?" Miz Willow peered at them.

"Taters keepin' warm on the stove next to the stew," Hattie said readily. "Carrots are already boiled and in with the pot roast."

"Bread? Corn bread? Biscuits?" The old woman read off her list.

"Four loaves, one pan, and two batches waitin' in the breadbox," Daisy ticked off.

"Another loaf in the hearth nook, up in the wall jist high enough so the stove doesn't block it, and another pan finishin' in the new oven," Hattie added.

"Coffee cake?" Miz Willow was obviously determined not to miss a thing. "Apple pies?"

"Two cakes covered on the table." Hattie pointed. "One pie coolin' on the windersill, and another bakin' in the old ash oven."

"Anything I missed?" Miz Willow looked around in satisfaction.

"We've got cool fresh milk and lots of coffee for drinkin'," Daisy mused. "We set out half a barrel of apples in the shade. Butter and honey are covered and on the table, along with preserves. The egg salad is keepin' cool in the well."

"And I'll have the cheese sliced and on a platter before you know it," Hattie finished.

"Well, ladies." Miz Willow beamed a gummy smile. "I'd say we're ready for the onslaught."

"Yes, ma'am!" Daisy and Hattie exclaimed in tandem before collapsing onto the benches. They'd stayed up through most of the night getting all the food ready for the barn raising, but it would be worth it.

Daisy closed her eyes for a moment before pulling herself up again. "I'd better go get Jamie. I hope he slept all right in the barn loft with Bryce." She turned to Hattie. "It was good of Logan to spend the night up there with them, making it a boys' night."

"Yes." Hattie smiled. "Almost makes me feel bad I didn't make him a special breakfast!"

"I think he'll live." Daisy cast a glance around the food-filled cabin and shared a laugh with the other women before heading out to the barn.

She tapped hesitantly on the door. What if they weren't up and dressed yet? She rubbed her eyes while waiting.

"Good morning!" Bryce flung open the door, striding out with Jamie in one arm and the eggs they'd gathered in the other.

"Morn'g!" Jamie echoed.

"Good to see you!" Daisy bit back a yawn and swung Jamie into her arms. "My!" She hefted him up and down until he giggled. "I think you've gone and grown since I saw you last."

"Uh-huh!" Jamie grinned before planting a kiss on her cheek.

"Did you have fun with yore sleepover?" Daisy directed the question to Bryce.

"Yep." Bryce nudged Jamie's shoulder. "After working all day and tucking in to dinner last night, we all just fell into our beds and slept."

"Sounds lovely." Daisy stifled another yawn. "He wouldn't have gotten much sleep in the cabin last night — we were making such a racket getting things ready."

"Oh?" Bryce's close scrutiny made Daisy want to scurry back inside to wash her face and brush her hair. "Didn't you get to sleep at all last night?" His concern showed in an uncharacteristic frown.

"A bit." Daisy lightened her tone and smiled. "We snatched a few minutes here and there in shifts. We made shore Miz Willow drifted off more often than she told us to let her."

"Well." Bryce smoothly took Jamie from her. "I'd say you should go catch a few minutes more. Folks won't be showing up for another hour or so. I'll watch Jamie, and I'm sure Miz Willow has things under control. Why don't you and Hattie go to her room and snooze for a bit? I'll knock on the door to wake you up when it's time."

"Thankee, Bryce." Too tired to turn down the generous offer, Daisy smiled at him.

As she and Hattie snuggled into bed for a quick nap, Daisy thought of how natural Bryce looked with Jamie in his arms. It was the last image she remembered before drifting off into a sleep too deep for dreams.

Knock, knock, knock. The pesky sound wouldn't let up, no matter how deeply Daisy burrowed into the pillows.

It cain't be time to rise yet! I jist shut my eyes!

"Daisy?" Bryce's questioning rumble

caused her to open one eye.

Ooh. She swung her feet over the side of the bed and nudged Hattie. *Today's the barn raisin'. I wouldn't have had a wink of sleep iff'n it weren't for Bryce ordering me to sneak in a nap.*

"We're up!" Daisy called, reaching out for a deep stretch.

"All right." She heard him walk away.

"C'mon, Hattie." Daisy rubbed her friend's shoulder. "People are comin' for the barn raisin'."

"What?" Hattie sat bolt upright. "Oh! We'd better get goin'!" She scrambled out of bed and tossed Daisy the only other dress she owned. They quickly donned the fresh clothes and splashed their faces with cold water.

"Mercy." Daisy stared at her hair in horror. "Did I look like this before I went to fetch Jamie this mornin'?" she demanded of Hattie.

"Not quite," Hattie responded loyally, swiftly plaiting her hair into one long braid down her back. "But jist 'bout."

"How could you let me step foot outside lookin' a fright," Daisy wailed, hastily pulling the pins from her tresses.

"I look 'bout the same." A sly grin spread across Hattie's face. "Who're you tryin' to impress? Cain't be me, Miz Willow, Jamie, or Logan." She intentionally left out the only other person on the property that morning.

"Hobble yore mouth, Hattie!" Daisy raked her fingers through the worst of the snarls. "It ain't that I have anyone to impress. It's a matter of being ladylike!" *Though I don't want Bryce seein' me all disheveled.*

"Shore." Hattie drew out the word as she handed her friend the brush. "Well, whatever it is, you better hurry. I hear some folks startin' to arrive."

"No!" Daisy gasped, staring at her reflection in dismay. She finished brushing her hair and made a quick decision. She didn't have time to do anything but one long braid like Hattie's. *I cain get the snarls out, but how am I ever gonna get that man out of my hair?*

Within a matter of minutes, the homestead went from empty to teeming with neighbors. Bryce stood alongside Logan and greeted everybody who pulled up, taking the horses over to the hitching posts they'd put up just for the day.

"Good to see you, Bryce." Asa Pleasant slapped him on the shoulder. "Glad to see you haven't left us just yet."

"I wouldn't miss this," Bryce answered. Asa was a good man — uncle — to Eunice and Lois, two of the MacPhersons' brides. But that was a story in and of itself. For now, Bryce was glad to see such a talented worker here to help raise the barn. Asa was one of the local carvers whose work Logan sold to a dealer in Louisville. Asa Pleasant's swan-neck wall hooks and hand-carved nativity sets were nothing less than works of art.

"Hey, Bryce!" Ted Trevor stood before him.

"Hello, Ted." Bryce looked around for Ted's twin brother. "Where's Fred?"

"He's around here somewhere." Ted shrugged. "Listen, we've whatcha call a minor disagreement you cain settle for us."

"Oh?" The comment piqued Bryce's interest.

"Most folks we've grown up with cain't tell the two of us apart, but you don't seem to have no trouble." Ted grinned. "I say it's 'cuz you noticed that I'm taller, but Fred is of the opinion that he's the handsome one. What's the reason?"

"Wait a minute!" Fred came dashing up alongside his brother. "You cain't ask him less'n we're both in front of him." He puffed out his chest, and Ted stood up as straight as he could and craned his neck. "All right. We're ready."

"Sorry, fellas," Bryce apologized. "But you're like two peas in a pod. Neither one is taller or shorter or more handsome."

"But I've only had my nose broke once!" Fred scowled at Bryce.

"Only on account of you bein' too lily-livered to climb that rockfall," Ted retorted.

"You mean havin' the good sense not to!" Fred shot back before they both looked at Bryce again. "So how cain you tell?"

"Fred has a scar on his right hand that you don't, Ted." Bryce watched both their faces crumple in identical disappointment. "But listen, I've got five brothers, and Logan's the one who looks least like me. People get us mixed up all the time back home. Don't mean a thing unless you let it."

"Right. So I'm the brave one," Ted crowed.

"And I'm the one with more sense than God gave a goat," Fred added. The two brothers shared a grin.

"Good enough." They spoke in tandem. "Thanks, Bryce!"

He watched as the two scampered off to get into some new mischief. The Trevor twins were three years younger than Logan, and Bryce had five on the pair of 'em. They were a rambunctious set but had their hearts in the right place.

"Bryce!" Ed Trevor, father to the twins, headed his way. "Jist the man I wanted to see!"

"How are you, Ed?" Bryce liked the good-natured hound-dog breeder.

"Wondered if you could see yore way clear to comin' down after church tomorrow. One of my older dogs whelped unexpected, and the litter came late, too. One of the dogs's a runt, too scrawny to make it through winter as is."

"I'll see what I can do, Ed." Depended on how strong the critter was. "What makes you think it'll be such a bad winter?"

"Spring came early this year, so the winter'll be rough. 'Sides, dogs' coats are comin' in extry thick. Gearin' up for the cold. God takes care of critters like that."

"Good thing we're getting this done today." Bryce spotted Otis Nye struggling to walk with his cane while carrying a sack. He quickly took the sack from the old man. "Where does this go?"

"To wherever yore puttin' the vittles." Otis thumped his cane for emphasis. "That's a ham."

"I'll take it to the kitchen for the women to decide where it goes," Bryce offered.

Otis nodded as he plunked himself down on a bench. "Good thing you and that brother of yourn didn't wait any longer for this barn. Gonna be a rough winter — I cain feel it in my bones. What're you waitin' for, boy?" Otis waved Bryce off. "Get goin'!"

Bryce pushed toward the cabin through what he thought of as a veritable herd of women. *No, wait a minute. I can't talk about women like that,* Bryce reminded himself, *even if they are all gathered in one nearly impenetrable mass, jabbering on and getting in my way. Would "flock" be any better? They do chatter and cluck like birds. No, I don't think they'd appreciate that, either.*

Bryce shook his head as he waded through the plumage — really, one of the women had droopy feathers on her hat that tickled his nose when he walked by. Women stumped him. If only all of them were as easy to be around as —

"Daisy!" He called her name as he saw her making her way into the cabin.

"Yes, Bryce?" She stopped. He loved to hear the sound of his name on her lips. She said it soft and careful, not short and clipped like so many others.

"Otis brought a ham." Bryce lifted the sack. "Where do you want me to put it?"

"I'll take it." Daisy reached out, and he

slid it into her arms, his fingertips tingling as they brushed against hers.

Chapter 13

Daisy carried the sack inside, winding her way through the crush of people.

"I done brought you two roast chickens." Silk Trevor pointed to where she'd laid them out on the table. "Nice thang is, they cain be jist as good et cold."

"Thankee, Silk." Miz Willow rocked contentedly in her chair.

"We brung salad filled with vegetables we grew!" Young Lark Cleary plunked the bowl down.

"I cain't think on another thing we ain't got already," Hattie mused. "Look at that spread!"

"One more thing." Daisy grunted as she slid the bag onto the table bench. "Otis Nye sent this here ham."

"We'd best get to carvin' it then." Hattie handed Daisy a big, shiny new knife. "The barn raisin'll begin any minute now, and we don't want to miss it!"

I ain't so shore about that, Daisy disagreed. *The last time I attended a barn raisin', Peter worked alongside these men. His blond hair won't catch my eye in the crowd today. I won't have a man to take water to and smile with.* She bowed her head for a moment. *These women all around either don't know me or feel sorry for me. I cain't spend the day jabbering with them. I hate when Jamie and me don't have a place at big get-togethers. So many others don't know how to treat Jamie. When they talk at him like he's a baby, it cuts him deep. I know they don't understand that his mind's as sharp as this knife even though his words come out garbled, but that don't make it hurt any less.*

Daisy took a deep breath, relieved that the women had left the cabin. People would be pressing in on her, around her, all day. Normally that didn't get her goat, but since she didn't feel able to join in the conversation, it made her feel insignificant. *Invisible.* She'd rather be alone in the cabin working than with ten other women and just standing there with nothing to say or do.

"None of that now." Miz Willow's order cracked Daisy's thoughts.

"What? Am I doing this wrong?" She looked down at the platter of ham she hadn't been paying close enough attention to, but it seemed fine to her.

"Yore doin' somethin' wrong, child. But it ain't the ham." Miz Willow came close to stand beside her. "Yore cutting yoreself off from others before the day's begun."

"I'm not cutting myself off," Daisy denied. "I don't have to prove anything to these people. They all seem so nice, but I know what's under it." She squared her shoulders. "Jamie and me don't need their pity."

"That's jist what I mean," Miz Willow declared. "Yore rejecting the folk around here without even trying. You been cut off so long at Hawk's Fall, busy with Jamie, you ain't spent much time with others. You know a lot of these people. It ain't been five years since you moved from Salt Lick Holler with yore husband."

"Six." Daisy's voice cracked. *And nearly five of being alone. Taking the responsibility for a household and my son.*

"And now, here you are surrounded by good people. Are you talkin' to any of 'em?" Miz Willow demanded. "No. Yore retreating in silence while that attitude jist rolls outta you."

"What attitude? I'm simply minding my own business."

" 'Zactly. You mind yore own business and expect ev'rybody else to mind theirs." Miz

Willow kept on. "So you tell yoreself how you and Jamie don't need folks' pity. How do you know they pity you? Do you pity yoreself?"

"No! I've worked hard for what Jamie and I got."

"Yore full of pride at yore own self-reliance, Daisy. You don't open yore heart and let people care about you." Miz Willow rested a hand on Daisy's shoulder. "We've all known loss, Daisy. We all need something."

"We lost our home, but we'll still make our way." Daisy spoke aloud the words she lived by. "We survive no matter what."

"Let me tell you somethin' I've learned from bein' around longer than yore pa cain remember." Miz Willow headed for the door. "Survivin' ain't livin'."

Bryce looked around. The Trevors, Pleasants, Peasleys, Ruckers, and Clearys had all shown up, along with some faces he recognized but couldn't put a name to.

"Looks like we're about to begin." Bryce found Logan, who was clanging a cowbell to get everybody's attention.

"All right. Looks like everybody made it." Logan surveyed the crowd with satisfaction. "I'd like to thank you all for comin' here today to help us raise this barn. I know it's a bit late in the year, but together we can get this done!" A few calls and whoops of agreement filled the air as he paused.

"We need the barn for the horses and cattle I'm having brought up. Now that I've decided to stay in Salt Lick Holler with my beautiful bride, Hattie." He stopped to blow Hattie a kiss. She blushed scarlet and motioned for him to continue.

"I'm fixing to set us up with my share of Chance Ranch. So it seems to me that you fine folks who're helping us out deserve something in return." While Logan paused to let that sink in, Bryce marveled at his brother's dramatic flair.

"We're asking the men to divide into teams. We're building on to the existing barn, so we'll have three walls. That means three teams. Bryce and I will make up one team — it's only fair we put up at least one of these walls! That means we need two more. When you have your teams together, Miz Willow will write your names down. First team to construct their wall wins the little mare." Logan pointed to the pretty brown pony tied to a post. The rest of the animals were grazing in makeshift corrals over the hill. The hastily made fences wouldn't hold them for too long, but they wouldn't have to after today.

Murmurs of surprise and excitement filled the air as people sought out friends to form teams.

"We've got a team right here, Logan!" Ed Trevor waved his hammer in the air. "Me, m' boys, and their uncle Asa." He turned to the crowd. "And we aim to win that pony!"

"Not if we have anything to say about it!" Nate Rucker called out the names of the men on his team.

"All right then. Otis Nye'll be our judge. Watch yourselves. He's got the keenest eyes in the holler." Logan set out the rules, listed the dimensions of the walls, and explained how the lumber had already been divided. "Everybody ready? Let's go!" The race was on. Bryce grabbed a bag of nails and strode up to Daisy.

"Our team's a bit short on manpower. How 'bout if you let Jamie here hold our tools for us so we can get to them real fast?"

"Shore thang." Daisy set Jamie down on a small patch of grass just outside of the range of swinging lumber. She sat down next to him and arranged the drills, saws, hammers, and such in front of them where it would be easy for Bryce and Logan to see them. "Thanks, buddy." Bryce winked at Jamie and Daisy and ran to help Logan heft the lumber. They were already behind, but that didn't matter. He didn't aim to win this race.

I don't want the pony. Bryce glanced over at Daisy and Jamie. *I've got my eyes on a sweet little filly who's a much finer prize. Too bad she's so dead set on running the other way.*

"And the winner is . . . ," Otis Nye bellowed grandly, "team two! Ed, Ted, Fred, and Asa win the pony!"

"Yea!" Ted jumped in the air while Fred whooped. The rest of the men grumbled good-naturedly and threw a few overblown glowers toward the winners.

"That don't mean yore done, men!" Otis squawked. "Everybody get back to work!"

Ted and Fred joined Logan and Bryce, who lagged far behind, in part because it was just the two of them but also because they'd taken on the wall with the door, which made things more complicated. With the extra help, they began to catch up. The twins proved to be nimble climbers and swift workers as they poured all their considerable energy into the task at hand.

The scent of fresh sawdust coated the air as hammers rang and saws scraped. Men yelled back and forth for whatever they happened to need at the moment. Occasional "ows" punctuated the rhythm of hard work. The women drifted around the work site with fresh water to drink and cool rags to mop overheated brows.

"Nails." Bryce took the small pouch from Jamie's hand and traded him an empty one. Daisy filled the small pouches so Jamie didn't ever touch the sharp points of the nails. "Thanks, buddy. We make a good team."

He rushed back to lift a heavy piece of timber with Logan. They'd nearly finished constructing the bents; now they'd need to raise the skeleton of the wall. He looped a strong rope around the topmost bar while Logan did the same. The twins were ready with the long, spiked stockades to brace the fledgling structure while Logan and Bryce pulled it upright.

His muscles strained at the weight. If this barn were any bigger, he and Logan couldn't have raised this wall even with the twins' assistance. Nate Rucker ambled over and grabbed an extra rope Bryce had thought to tie in case one gave way. With the help of the burly blacksmith, the frame rose far more quickly.

"Thanks, Nate." Bryce grinned at the enormous man, affectionately called "Li'l

Nate" because his father, the blacksmith of the holler before him, was "Big Nate." Bryce had been in the holler for just a few days when Li'l Nate's wife, Abigail, bore him a son. Bitty Nate looked to be taking after his pa already.

"Any time," Nate grunted, holding tight while others rushed over to help secure the frame. Finally, they could let go.

Bryce gave a mighty stretch to work out the kinks. He took a few deep breaths, fanning himself with his hat.

"Have some water." Daisy's voice floated to his ears as she walked toward him.

"Much obliged." Bryce took the cool drink and downed it in three gulps. "Ah. That's better."

"I cain get some more," she offered. "Yore working terrible fast."

"I'm fine." He grinned at her. *She's been watching me.* The thought took his mind off his weary muscles.

"I wanted to thank you." Daisy leaned close enough that he could smell the fancy soap she used. "For includin' Jamie. It meant a lot that he got to holp the men instead of only watching."

"And help us he did. You, too. Having everything at the ready made things that much easier." Bryce slapped his hat back on his head and tipped the brim toward her. "I've got to get back to work. We've got to get the rafters up before dinner, and I'm mighty hungry."

"You always are!" Daisy's laugh followed him as he joined the other men.

Daisy got some more water and brought it to Jamie. She tipped the cup to his lips. Usually he could do it, but today he'd already used a lot of his strength. She wiped his chin and cuddled him close.

She knew he was tired but didn't press him. He wouldn't doze off until after the rafters had been raised and he had a belly full of lunch. Daisy hummed softly as she ran her fingers through his soft blond hair, so like his father's.

She raised her head to see Miz Willow watching her. A surge of anger at the old woman's scolding welled up.

How dare she criticize the way I behave! Daisy stewed. *I know I'm beholden to her for her hospitality, but I don't intend for it to be permanent. Does sharing her home give her the right to berate me for nothing? I don't cut myself off from others. I've established a friendship with Bryce, haven't I?*

Only in spite of yourself. Daisy didn't like the niggling voice in the back of her mind, but the tiny seeds of guilt wouldn't rest. *You didn't reach out to Bryce until he was kind to Jamie. Even then, you accused him of cruelty not in his nature. If the friendship has grown, it is not due to yore tender care in nurturing it. Miz Willow said those things to open yore eyes, not to hurt you.*

Well, she did hurt me. And if she feels that I'm so difficult, it's all the better that I've taken Logan up on his offer to sell my lace. His deal puts far more money in my pocket. The more I save, the sooner I cain leave the old woman's charity, and me and Jamie cain get on with our lives.

I've wasted too much time already. After the fire, we spent two days searching the rubble before moving here. Sewing new clothes was necessary but cost me a lot of time, and holping with that behemoth of a stove ate up still more time. I need to focus on the important things. How am I going to put a roof over Jamie's head and food in his mouth? By making lace. That's how I should be spending my time. Her resolve strengthened, Daisy vowed to work more quickly.

While she'd been lost in thought, the men had finished putting up half of the rafters. The noontime hour had passed, so when the skeleton of the barn was up and ready, everyone would break for dinner.

"Mama's gonna go set out the food," Daisy told Jamie. "I want you to stay right here where I cain see you, okay?"

" 'Kay, Ma." He nodded, happy to be watching everything around him.

Daisy walked over to the cabin and began carrying out dish after covered dish. They hadn't set it all outside before now, so the sun wouldn't spoil the food and insects wouldn't swarm around the tables. Logan and Bryce had constructed two huge tables and numerous benches in preparation for the day.

Daisy, Hattie, Silk Trevor, and a few other women scurried back and forth while Miz Willow passed them dishes. Before long, the first table groaned beneath the weight of sliced ham, a pot roast, two chickens, rabbit stew, egg salad, vegetable salad, mashed potatoes, gravy, steamed carrots, and hunks of cheese. Baked goods filled the second table to bursting. Bread, rolls, biscuits, corn bread, pies, coffee cake, and cobbler spread in a tantalizing profusion.

Logan called for silence before blessing the meal.

"We're going to take a minute to thank the Lord for the food and friends gathered today.

"Lord, I thank You for each person here

today. Every one of them has things they need to be attending to, but they've taken the time to come and help me and Hattie and Miz Willow build a bigger barn. Thank You for the food on the tables. We ask that You bless it so we have the strength to finish our work today. You've provided graciously for us, and we ask You to shed Your blessings on the people here today. In Your name. Amen."

The smell of savory meat mixed with the earthy fragrance of baked cinnamon as the men gathered around to fill their plates. Daisy couldn't remember ever seeing so much food, much less watching it all disappear so quickly. After the men hunkered down, their plates piled high with food, the women and children swarmed around the tables.

"Here, Jamie." Daisy returned to find Bryce sitting with her son. Jamie nibbled on a chicken leg while Bryce attacked a mound of mashed potatoes. Daisy sat down and put Jamie's plate in easy reach. "How're them taters, Bryce?"

"Good." Bryce barely stopped eating long enough to grunt his approval.

" 'Ood." Jamie nodded, waving his piece of chicken.

Daisy's heart twisted. *Jamie used to copy-*

cat me like that. Now he's apin' Bryce. Lord, why do I feel as though that's a loss? Bryce has become so important to my son, but he'll be gone all too soon. What am I to do?

Chapter 14

"I've put the axes and saws in the back of the wagon." Logan sauntered into the cabin two days later and tried to peek in the lunch basket the women had packed.

Daisy chuckled when Hattie swatted his hand away.

"I have the horses hitched." Bryce came in behind his brother. "What's the holdup? We've got to get going if we're going to chop enough before dark."

"Here you go." Daisy handed the basket to Bryce while Logan wolfed down a leftover biscuit.

"Thanks, Daisy." Bryce's rugged smile made it difficult for Daisy not to stare.

"Yore welcome." She stepped back. "A man needs plenty in his belly so's he cain get a lot done."

"Me man!" Jamie scooched over and jabbed his chest. "I go?"

No. Not a chance. Not even with two

Chances. They'll be fellin' deadwood — ain't safe for any child, much less my son! Jist the thought of that two-man saw makes me wanna hold Jamie close and never let him go.

Daisy bit back the words, knowing how hurt Jamie would be if she explained it like that. She scrambled to concoct a reason to refuse.

"Of course you're a man," Logan proclaimed.

Oh no. He's going to say yes. Logan'll let Jamie tag along, and then summat terrible'll happen. Daisy chewed the inside of her lip. *A deadwood branch cain fall, a blade might be left unattended, a shift in the wind so a felled tree goes the wrong way . . . And I cain't think up an excuse to tell them all no. What do I do? I cain't let him go!*

She saw Bryce bending over to talk to Jamie. *No, Bryce! You've let Jamie do so many things already. I was wrong about the eggs and the leaves but not this. Don't take Jamie where he cain't be safe. You must have the sense to know this won't end well. Don't make me let loose the words that will shame my son afore you and yore brother.*

"Not today, buddy."

Thankee, Bryce. Daisy took a calming breath. *Jamie'll be safe. I was so worried.*

Bryce squatted down to look Jamie in the

eye. "We need you to stay here and keep watch on things for us. We're chopping enough wood to fill the whole wagon before we bring it back. The pieces'll be so long." He spread his arms wide. "We'll have to make 'em smaller tomorrow. Then you'll be right there with us. Fair enough?"

More than fair. You found a way to protect my son and still make him part of the task.

" 'Kay." Jamie puffed out his chest. " 'Morra I holp."

"But today yore going to holp yore mama!" Daisy gathered him in her arms. "We've got lots of thangs to get done afore Logan and Bryce come back!" She smiled at Bryce, hoping he understood that she meant to thank him for protecting Jamie but not treating him like a baby. He was so good with her and Jamie. *Yep. Bryce Chance jist has a way of makin' a body feel special.*

Bryce pitched a forkful of hay into one of the new stalls. Logan was setting up tack.

"I think we should keep the cattle in the old half and the horses in the new," Bryce planned aloud.

"Makes sense to have the horses on hand," Logan agreed. "Seemed like everyone I talked with is preparing for a rough winter."

"Heard about Otis Nye's bones, did you?"

Bryce grinned.

"And how spring came early." Logan grabbed a pitchfork and started spreading hay around. They'd transfer the animals the next day. "Ed Trevor mentioned something about the hounds having thick coats."

"I heard the same thing. That reminds me." Bryce leaned on his pitchfork. "After we get the animals settled in tomorrow morning, I need to go to the Trevor place. Has a runt no one's spoken for. All the others have homes lined up."

Logan shrugged. "If it's made it this long, I think it's got a good chance of growing."

"Not with winter coming on fast." Bryce shook his head. "He won't have enough meat on his bones to get through the cold."

"That's rough," Logan commiserated. "How did it happen that Ed got in such a late litter?"

"Happens sometimes." Bryce thought a moment. "Ed said something about her being one of his older breeders."

"What are you going to do with the pup?" Logan asked.

"I won't know until I see it. Might be it just needs some extra attention and some cow's milk to fatten it up. It's worked before. Ed has too many dogs to spend that much time on a runt. Maybe I can take it off his hands."

"Oh?"

Something about Logan's tone raised Bryce's hackles. "You got something to say?"

"How are you going to manage a pup on your five-day, cross-country train trek?" Logan drummed his fingers against one of the new walls.

"Might be a bit of a problem," Bryce admitted.

"You could stay through the winter." Logan got the words out in a rush.

"I've been away from the ranch for six months already. You want me to sleep out in the barn through a mountain winter?"

"I have it on good authority that this is a mighty fine barn! You could use the tack room so the smell won't get to you. We both know that the animals will put off enough heat to keep the place warm."

"For the sake of a little dog?" Bryce shook his head. "You can feed the thing without me."

"I was thinking you might have other reasons to stay." Logan waggled his brows. "I saw you eating lunch with Daisy the other day. She's a fine woman."

"Yes, she is." Bryce set to work again and avoided his brother's piercing gaze. "But that doesn't amount to a hill o' beans. She's dead set on rebuilding the home and life she and her son lost. Even if I stayed the winter, I would eventually go back to Chance Ranch. Daisy's already lost too much to give up anything more."

"I see you've given this some thought, but did you think about all she stands to gain? You two seem to enjoy each other's company, and you get on well with Jamie."

"He's a great kid." Bryce chewed the inside of his cheek. "But I can't leave Chance Ranch shorthanded this winter to pursue a woman who has other plans."

"Are you so sure she wouldn't give up those plans?"

"She's a good friend, Logan, but she's a mother first," Bryce tried to explain. "Jamie's welfare is the only thing she's interested in."

"So how come she smiles at you like that and brings you water and makes sure we have something for dessert every night, if it's not because she likes you and noticed your sweet tooth?"

"She's a thoughtful woman." Bryce tried not to let Logan's words sink in. False hopes never made a man anything but wrong.

"Hattie's of the opinion that Daisy's thinking, all right." Logan paused meaningfully. "On you."

"You talked to Hattie about this?" Bryce practically bellowed the words.

"She brought up how much time Daisy spent with you while we were gone," Logan said casually, "and we've both kept an eye on the pair of you. Hattie thinks you two have something, and I agree."

Could that be true? Is Daisy interested in me the way I'm attracted to her? There were those times when we touched — she seemed flustered. Could there be room enough in her heart for a new husband? I care for Jamie a great deal, and I'd treat him as my own son. Would Daisy be willing to come with me to California?

"I can see the questions rolling about in your head, Bryce." Logan stared at him long and hard. "Are you willing to give up a winter to find the answers?"

Daisy looked up as Bryce entered the cabin. The determined set of his jaw as he strode across the room sent a chill down her spine. She rested her lacework in her lap and waited. Whatever it was he had to say, it must be important. Could something be wrong with the new barn? Then he stopped in front of her.

"Daisy Thales, I've made a decision." The intensity of his gaze stirred something deep within her.

"What is it, Bryce?"

"I'm staying through the winter."

What? No! How am I going to guard my heart against this man iff'n I cain't be shore he's leavin'? We'll be snowbound more often than not. He'll be here every time I turn around. What would make him change his mind? Why is he telling me and not Miz Willow and Hattie? What is he waiting for me to say?

Her breath caught at a possible answer. *He . . . he wouldn't be staying for me? Yes, I'm attracted to him — but does he feel the same way? About me? Plump, plain me with a son by another man? Only one way to find out.*

"What made you change yore mind?" She tried to keep her voice steady and light but failed miserably.

"You." He stepped forward and took her hand in his. Heat coursed through her fingers. "My mind's made up; I plan to court you, Daisy."

"Me?" The word came out as a squeak. She shook her head in disbelief, and his grip tightened as though he wouldn't let go.

"Don't say anything now. It's beginning stages yet, but I figured you deserved fair warning." He gave her palm a final squeeze.

"Good night."

Daisy watched, dumbfounded, as he left. She stared down at her hand, still tingling from the warmth of his. She leaned back before she registered Hattie and Miz Willow staring avidly. *At least Jamie's already fast asleep!*

She opened her mouth, realized she had no idea what to say, and cleared her throat instead. *I cain't believe it. I got no choice but to believe it. I don't even have time to work it through in my head 'cuz the man didn't have the sense God gave a flea. He tromped in, made his declaration in front of Miz Willow and Hattie, and took off. What am I supposed to say?*

"Well?" Hattie prompted, leaning forward in anticipation.

"Well, what?" Daisy picked up a piece of lacework to keep her hands busy.

"Put that stitchin' down, missy," Miz Willow ordered. "You've got some thinking to do, and yore gonna need some wise counsel."

I ain't ready for counsel, Daisy rebelled. *I don't know what to say! How cain you not see that?*

"Daisy?" Hattie caught her attention. "Do you not have any thoughts on what Bryce jist said?"

"I've got too many," Daisy moaned, burying her face in her hands. "And not a-one of 'em makes a lick of sense!"

"Then let's make sense out of it," Hattie declared firmly. "Now, puttin' aside the fact that Bryce surprised you, we have to remember that it's what he said that's important. Not the time or way he chose to say it."

"He could've spoke to me in private," Daisy muttered. *At least then I'd have my wits about me before I had to talk it over.*

"That probably would've been best," Miz Willow agreed. Her blue eyes crinkled with amusement. "But then Hattie and I would've been left out of the fun!"

"Never you mind 'bout that." Hattie swatted away Miz Willow's entertained cackle. "We ain't gonna tell anybody yore business, Daisy. What's important is whether or not yore interested in that buck." She eyed Daisy shrewdly. "I think you are, but yore the only one as knows for shore."

"I — I might," Daisy admitted. "But he's so different from Peter."

"As well he should be." Miz Willow resumed rocking. "Iff'n he was too much like yore first husband, you'd be comparin' 'em all the time. Bryce is his own man. If you want him, you want him for who he is, not who he cain't never be."

Daisy nodded slowly. Peter would always be her first love, but that was the way he was frozen in her thoughts. She'd married at fifteen, been widowed a scant year later. Peter had never even seen his eighteenth year. How could she ever compare her childhood sweetheart with a strong, steady man like Bryce?

"Could you love him?" Hattie got to the heart of the matter. "If not, then nothin' else need be considered."

"I'm not shore." Daisy bit her lip. *Could I spend the rest of my life with Bryce Chance?*

"But yore not willing to say no," Miz Willow observed. "There's something in that. For what it's worth, I say let Bryce Chance court you. He's a strong man dedicated to the Lord. Comes from good stock, takes you to be more'n jist a pretty face, and he's good with little Jamie."

"I'll sleep on it," Daisy decided. It was all she could commit to at this point.

"You need to pray on it." Hattie walked over and wrapped her in a hug. "Give it to God."

Give it to God. Hattie's words echoed in Daisy's mind later that night as she tried vainly to sleep. *I've been on my own for so long. How cain I give up somethin' this important?*

CHAPTER 15

Bryce stared at the ceiling, unable to sleep. *What made me go in there and burst out with a declaration like that? I should've waited for a better time. No, how would I have known it was a better time? I had something to say. Best to be out with it.*

He recalled the expressions on Daisy's face: surprise, followed by a kind of heat deep within her eyes, only to be extinguished by confusion. *But not disgust or outrage. She feels something, but neither one of us knows what it is yet. I hope that by declaring my interest, I've made it easier for her to trust me. What do I do now? Wait for her response?*

Bryce shook his head in frustration. He'd put himself out there, and she could leave him twisting in the wind for as long as she needed to. Why did it all have to be so difficult?

Lord, I've prayed about my feelings for

Daisy. I've thought long and hard about what to do. When Logan passed on the word that she might return my interest, I took it as a sign that I should go after what I wanted. What I still want. You know the desire in my heart. If it is a mistake, if this is not the path You want me to take, let Daisy tell me soon enough for me to leave before winter. I know she's spent the past five years standing on her own, but You and I both know she doesn't have to. Whether or not You intend for her to be my wife, I ask that You work in her heart and remind her that she's never alone. You are always with us. In Your holy name. Amen.

Having cast his cares upon the Lord, Bryce finally closed his eyes. Whatever the outcome of his decision tonight, he was sure he'd need to be well rested to face what lay ahead.

He awoke the next morning refreshed. After milking the cows — there were two dairy cows now in the extended barn — he headed for the cabin. He knocked lightly at the door, waiting for the go-ahead to step inside.

"Come on in." Miz Willow's voice came through the door, slightly muffled.

Bryce entered and set the milk on the table. Daisy stood before the stove, her back to him. It wasn't the welcome he'd hoped for, but he'd known Daisy might refuse him. Still, he took a deep breath before greeting her.

"Good morning, Daisy." He stepped close, lingering beside her a moment before picking up Jamie.

"Mornin'," Daisy spoke softly, but he heard it.

"Jamie and I'll go gather eggs. We'll be back soon." He left, only realizing when he got to the barn that he'd left the basket inside. He improvised, grabbing a spare bucket from the wall.

"Wun," Jamie counted, placing the first egg carefully in the bucket. "Two." He reached in as far as he could. "Tree!"

"That's right!" Bryce affirmed. "Three. Now you've got one more. Do you remember what number that is?"

"Umm . . ." Jamie scrunched his face in concentration.

"How old are you, Jamie?" Bryce shifted the egg pail to hang on the arm holding the boy. He held up his left hand and splayed four fingers. "This many, right?"

"Yes." Jamie nodded and reached out to tap the fingers. "Wun, two, tree . . ." He paused and looked at the last digit in consternation.

Bryce waited. If Jamie couldn't remember, he'd admit it. Sometimes all it took was an extra minute, so no sense rushing it. Jamie was a smart kid.

"Four!" Jamie burst out the number in excitement. "Four eggs, me four." He pointed to himself proudly.

"Exactly!" That was enough for today. The boy could count to ten, but there was no sense pushing it. As Jamie's hands grew less steady, Bryce helped him gather the rest of the eggs.

They carried the eggs back inside. Logan and Hattie were up and moving around. Suddenly, the cabin seemed too crowded. Bryce tried to catch Daisy's attention, but she kept busy until they sat down for breakfast. As Logan said grace, Bryce silently offered a prayer of his own.

Father, forgive me my impatience. Perhaps she needs time to think it over. I'm asking her to consider me as a husband, to decide whether she could move to California if the answer is yes. That's a lot to expect her to answer after one night's thought and prayer. But, Lord, I don't want to wait. Just seeing her and not knowing if this is as close as we can ever be is tearing me up. Give me patience and forbearance, Lord. Amen.

Daisy waited until Hattie and Miz Willow were checking their stock of yarbs and medicines for winter, then crouched down beside Jamie.

"Yore doin' real good with yore letters, Jamie. Mama wants you to keep practicing for a while. I'll be back in a little bit, understand?"

"Mm-hmm."

Daisy planted a quick kiss atop his golden head and slipped out of the cabin. She'd hardly taken three steps when Miz Willow's voice stopped her.

"C'mere and give an ole woman some of yore time," the healer instructed as she hobbled out of the house and took a seat on the porch.

Stifling a groan, Daisy sat down next to her.

"Now I know I ain't the person yore fixin' to talk with," Miz Willow began, "and I riled you the last time we spoke in private."

Daisy sat silently, not denying her words, but refusing to let Miz Willow know how angry she'd been.

"But I seen you all mornin' thinkin' so hard it's a wonder you got anythin' done."

The old woman held up her gnarled hands. "Not that I'm sayin' yore not a fine worker. Truth is, you've been a big holp 'round here, and I should have thanked you afore now."

"Yore kind enough to let me and my son stay in yore home." Daisy softened. "It's the least I cain do to see after a few chores."

"You've a good heart, Daisy Thales." Miz Willow tapped her cane on the porch. "I'd never say otherwise. But it's yore hard head we need to talk about." Daisy's back stiffened at the words, but the old woman plowed on ahead. "Try as I might, I cain't walk in yore shoes, Daisy. Bryce Chance is, as I said afore, a strong man of God, a fine provider, and a man who knows you better'n any other and wants to take care of you and yore son. I tried to wrap my mind around it, but I jist cain't seem to find the hitch. What're you caught on that I don't see?"

Miz Willow's voice had become tender, and she reached out to put an age-spotted hand atop Daisy's. The healer was trying to understand, and maybe voicing her fears would help Daisy allay them.

"First, it came as such a surprise, I couldn't see straight." Daisy tried to explain. "I've already married and lost the only man I ever loved. I didn't plan on loving another.

Doesn't it disrespect Peter's memory?"

"I don't think so." Miz Willow shook her head. "Yore not lookin' to replace yore childhood sweetheart, Daisy. You didn't set out to nab a husband. God put a fine man in yore path, and it does no discredit to Peter to find a husband for yoreself and a pa for young Jamie. The Bible even talks about how young widows should remarry.

"First Timothy, chapter 5, talks all about honorin' widows," Miz Willow added. " 'I will therefore that the younger women marry, bear children. . . .' "

"That holps a bit," Daisy admitted, breathing a little easier. "But that's jist part of it. I don't know if I cain love another man as a husband, and I don't want to encourage Bryce without cause."

"Sounds to me like yore putting the cart afore the mule, Daisy. He's taken a liking to you and yore boy. Yore not averse to him. He ain't popped the question yet, only said he wants to court you. Courtin's all 'bout findin' out whether or not you suit."

"Mayhap that's true. It's so different from afore. Peter and I growed up together, had a friendship that deepened and turned to love. It all came so natural." Daisy looked down at her hands. "Now it seems so forced. It's all up in the air with so many questions and no answers, and ev'rybody around is privy to the whole thing. What if he stays, and it don't work out? What will people think?"

"Why are you worried 'bout what goes on in the minds of others? Fretting 'bout yore standin' with others 'stead of wanting to foller God's will for yore life is a sure sign summat's sore wrong in yore heart and soul." Miz Willow stood up. "Would you rather not take the path God has put before you, not open yoreself to the chance of love, for the sake of avoiding a few gossips? If so, you don't deserve a man like Bryce Chance." She turned to go back inside. "Think on it, Daisy. Be shore you have the right reasons behind yore decision."

Cain't she see that's 'zactly what I'm tryin' to do? Talking with her don't make this any easier. The only person I should be talkin' this over with is Bryce. I don't know what I'll say, but we'll have to come to some sort of decision.

She hurried to the barn and eased the door open, checking to see if Bryce was tending to one of the animals as he did so often. Not seeing him, she made her way farther back, to the older half of the barn.

"He's not here." Logan's voice made her jump.

"You gave me a fright!" Daisy put a hand over her heart.

"Didn't mean to." Logan put down an empty water bucket beside a full trough and leaned against a post. "But like I said, Bryce isn't here."

"Oh?" Daisy tried to sound nonchalant but could see from the grin on Logan's face that she had failed abysmally.

"Yep." Logan finally took pity on her and broke the silence. "He went up to the Trevor place. He might not be back until suppertime. Something about an underweight pup."

"I see." *No, I don't! He laid all that on me last night and takes off the next morning? How am I supposed to sort out my feelings iff'n Bryce ain't even around?*

There it was. The answer she'd been looking for all night. Truth of the matter was, she did bear feelings for Bryce. Affection that could grow to love. But he had to be around for her to find out. *I want him to stay through the winter.* The knowledge both frightened and exhilarated her. *I'm not ready to promise anything, but I'm willing to give it a try.*

"Thanks, Logan." She smiled at him and started to leave.

"Wait a minute." Logan walked beside

her. "Is there a message you want me to pass on?"

"Nope." Daisy determined she'd talk to Bryce before anyone else. "I'll see you both at supper."

Logan looked at her as though trying to figure out what her decision would be, but Daisy didn't so much as lift an eyebrow. As she left the barn, she thought about the difference between the two brothers. Logan used words to understand and be understood. *Bryce would've knowed my answer just by looking at my face.*

"She's got spunk." Bryce laughed as the wriggly puppy burrowed a cold, wet nose into his neck. The ropy tail waved wildly, beating the air, Bryce's arms, and anything else within reach.

"Likes you," Ed noted. "Done everything I cain think on, but she's still a bitty li'l thang. Cain't sell her, that's for shore." He looked at the furry black-and-tan pup. "I make a habit of not keepin' the dogs inside. Coddles 'em too much, and then they're not as good for tracking. But this one might not have enough weight to make it through the winter."

"She needs fattening up. I'd give her cow's milk — as much as she'll take. I'd rest easier

if I knew she had a warm place to sleep."
Bryce pulled the puppy from where it was
climbing onto his shoulder. "Plenty of energy."

"I've got two late litters this year to look
after, and I'm behind on getting m' winter
firewood." Ed sighed. "I cain't be givin' this
one special treatment, and no one chose the
runt. Iff'n you want her, she's yores."

Bryce looked down at the small bundle of
fur currently burying her black nose in the
bend of his arm before sniffing her way over
to nuzzle at his buttons.

"I've got to go feed the breeders." Ed
shoved his hands in his pockets. "Get to
know her. I don't want you to take her and
regret it later. I'll be back in a bit."

"Sounds good." Bryce cradled the pup in
both palms and brought her to eye level.
Her tail thumped as she craned her neck to
poke his chin with an inquisitive snout.
"Snuffly little thing, aren't ya?"

*She's bitty now, and even after I get some
more weight on her, she'll never be as big as
her brothers and sisters. Ed's right — she
won't make the best hunting dog. Definitely
has the nose for it, though.*

Bryce cradled her close, and she buried
her face in his chest. He ran his fingertip
between her floppy ears.

*Friendly mite. She'd make a good compan-
ion — affectionate now, she'll be protective
once she's bigger. Every boy should have a
dog, and this one's tiny enough for Jamie to
hold now. They can grow a bit together, and
she'll look after him when she's older. Jamie
likes to feel things with his hands, and this
pup is soft and warm and cuddly. She won't
mind that he's a little clumsy. It'd do Jamie
good to have something to look after. Make
him feel important and capable.*

*Daisy might not like it at first, but she'll melt
when she sees the smile on Jamie's face
while he plays with his dog. I'll help him look
after the pup while she's small. She won't
need a lot of looking after when she's older —
food and water. Jamie'll give this pup all the
attention she needs, and she'll love him right
back. Dogs are loyal creatures.*

Bryce saw Ed coming back and gave the
pup a reassuring pat. It didn't seem right
that no one wanted her. He just couldn't
bring himself to leave her behind. "I'll look
after her, Ed. What's her name?"

"I don't know. I try not to name 'em, since
their owners like to do that. Then they cain't
get confused iff'n I train 'em under a different name and not come when they're
called." Ed thought a moment. "Since no
one paid for her, she don't have a name.

Reckon it's up to you. What'd you like to call her?"

Bryce looked down. Having tuckered herself out, she snuggled in his arms, pink tongue lolling out as she snoozed. She was a cute little thing. Her small black nose twitched in her sleep, and he could think of only one name that would do.

"Nosey."

CHAPTER 16

Daisy stared at the apple pie in dismay, its black edges and smoky scent declared it burned beyond redemption. She fanned a tea towel to wave the last few wisps of smoke out the door. She'd need to clean out the new oven.

I must've put too much wood in the stove and got the oven hotter'n it should be. I'm right glad Miz Willow and Hattie are at the Ruckers' so they don't see this. I cain't believe we managed all the victuals for the barn raisin' with nary a single problem, and now I done ruint the dessert I made to tell Bryce I'm glad he's staying. I ain't got time to make another!

"Well, Jamie," she sighed aloud, even though Jamie was napping, "that plan went up in smoke."

"What went up in smoke?" Bryce sniffed the singed air as he walked into the cabin.

No! Daisy couldn't let loose the howl that rose in her chest. *Yore not supposed to see*

*me like this — hair all flyaway, face flushed
from the stove, spots all over my apron . . .
and a burned apple pie on the windersill.* She
took a deep breath, realizing Bryce waited
for her to say something.

"I baked you an apple pie, but it came out
more burnt than anything I'd ask a body to
et." She flapped the towel toward the window, as much to point at the tart as to vent
some of her frustration. "I made the new
stove oven too hot."

"Looks fine to me." Bryce picked up the
still-warm tin, set it on the table, and
grabbed a fork.

"What're you doin'?" Daisy protested as
he plunged the fork into the middle of the
charred dessert.

"The edges are . . ." Bryce took another
bite and swallowed before continuing.
"Crispy. That I'll grant you. But it's not
ruined. The middle's wonderful." He
speared a spiced apple slice and held it to
her lips. "Taste."

"I —" She didn't get a word out before he
slipped the bite into her mouth.

"Got a speck here." Bryce's finger brushed
her lip tenderly. Warmth spread through her.

"See?" Bryce kept on eating. "Delicious."

That shore was. Daisy resisted the urge to
touch where his fingertip had brushed her

mouth. "You didn't have to do that."

"I know." Bryce held her gaze steadily. "I wanted to." Tension spread between them, tight and warm, before he lightened his tone. "Burnt offerings pleased God, and now I know why." He polished off the rest of the pie, leaving behind only the black edges.

Daisy shook her head and smiled at him, reaching for the tin. It'd have to be scrubbed. He gently caught her wrist.

"Leave it." He rose to his feet and started for the door, not loosening his hold. "I want to show you something."

"What?" Daisy glanced back at Jamie, still asleep on the bed.

"It's a surprise." He released her hand. "I'll bring it to you if you'd be more comfortable."

"I'll go." His consideration immediately made her relax. Besides, she'd been wanting to talk with him in private. Jamie would be fine, and this way she and Bryce could figure a few things out without her son overhearing the conversation. She followed Bryce out to the barn, and he led her to the tack room.

"Hold out your hands, Daisy," he instructed. "Now close your eyes."

Daisy did as he said, resisting the urge to

169

peek through her lashes as he put something small and soft in her palms. Something cold and wet snuffled her hand, and she would have dropped it had Bryce not cupped her hands in his.

"Open 'em."

She looked down. "Oh!" She cradled the tiniest puppy she'd ever seen. Daisy lifted it up to get a better look, and the pup bumped her nose with its. She giggled as the pup nosed its way over her face, the soft fur tickling her skin.

Although mostly black, tan markings decorated the fur around its eyes, paws, and the tip of its tail, which wagged enthusiastically.

"I cain't recollect the last time I saw such a cute critter," Daisy marveled. When Bryce stepped back, she cuddled the puppy close. It immediately poked at her stomach with its nose, snuffling excitedly. "Curious li'l thang."

"I've named her Nosey." Bryce reached out and stroked the soft black fur.

"Fits her." Daisy laughed. *But why are you showing her to me? Is she a gift?* There was no denying the little pup had winning ways, but the last thing Daisy needed was another mouth to feed.

"Yep." Bryce waited for her to look up

from the furry bundle before speaking again. "She's a runt, and Ed Trevor doesn't have the time to look after her like she needs. I'll be feeding her cow's milk so she bulks up for the winter."

"I'm glad. She's too friendly and precious not to be loved." Daisy smiled her approval. *And how wonderful it is that you care enough to bring her home.* "You've got a fine heart, Bryce Chance." *Do you understand what I'm saying?*

"Every boy needs a dog." He looked her in the eye, then said, "I was hoping . . . Jamie could help me with her." Bryce asked her more than one question with that statement.

"He'd like that," Daisy answered, pausing for a moment before adding softly, "and so would I."

"Thank you, Daisy." A grin split across his face. "So you're all right with me staying?"

"Yes, Bryce." She nodded but became serious. "But I want to make a few things clear."

"I'm listening." Bryce reached for the puppy and leaned forward to catch her words.

"I'm not committing to anything jist yet. I don't know iff'n this whole thang'll work out, but I want to try."

"That's all I'm asking for, Daisy. A chance to spend more time with you and Jamie to see where it leads."

His words lifted a load off her shoulders.

"Then we're agreed. Yore staying but no promises." Daisy had to make sure she wasn't misleading him.

"Yep. And I want you to know that I care for Jamie in his own right, not only because he's your son." Bryce alleviated a concern Daisy had left unspoken. "I'm courting you with an eye to becoming part of a family, not just a husband."

Daisy didn't say another word, but her eyes shone with relief. Bryce knew she wouldn't have agreed to step out with him unless she already knew he'd care for Jamie, but he wanted her to hear the words and know how deeply he meant it.

"I've got to go wake Jamie, else he won't sleep through the night." Daisy passed Nosey back to him.

"Why don't we let Nosey wake him?" Bryce suggested, keeping apace with her. "That cold nose of hers would make a fine wake-up call."

"Sounds like fun."

They tiptoed into the cabin and snuck up

near the bed. Bryce reached out and deposited the dog beside the sleeping boy, then watched and waited. Sure enough, Nosey stood up, placed one dainty paw on Jamie's chest, and buried her wet nose under his chin.

"Huh?" Jamie looked up at them with bleary eyes before tilting his head and seeing what had woken him up. "Puppy!" He sat up straight and scooped the puppy into his arms. She thumped her tail so fast it became a blur while she covered his face with doggy kisses. Jamie giggled. "Mine?" he asked excitedly.

Bryce looked at Daisy. She sent him a brief nod, and they answered together. "Yours."

They watched the little boy play with the puppy, who sniffed him, the pillow, the blankets — anything and everything around her.

I understand, Nosey. Bryce couldn't stop grinning if his life depended on it. *I'm testing the air, too. If we play our cards right, we'll both have a new family.* He glanced at the window as a sudden cloud cast the sun in shadow. *I hope it's a long winter.*

"I et too much." Daisy leaned back on the tattered quilt and put her hand on her stomach. The sun shone down on the folks gathered for the Harvest Games and Picnic.

"Me, too." Bryce stretched out beside her on the grass. "I couldn't fit in another bite."

"So you don't want the pie I brought you?" Logan flopped down, passing Hattie a piece of apple pie that Daisy had baked for the day before tackling a wedge of his own.

"Aw . . . my favorite." Bryce looked longingly at the dessert before him.

Even Daisy's mouth watered at the tantalizing aroma of apples and cinnamon. *At least this one turned out right. The last one I baked all but burnt to a crisp, and Bryce et it anyhow.*

"Maybe one small bite . . ." Bryce jabbed his fork into the treat and chewed the first bite. "Mmm. Nope. I need another taste." He closed his eyes as he savored the next bite. "I can tell Daisy baked this." He opened his eyes, held her gaze, and lowered his voice. "It tastes like cinnamon, sugar, and sweetness."

"Oh?" Daisy tried to be nonchalant but felt the blush beginning anyway. She nabbed his fork. "Guess I'd better try some of that myself then!" Together they polished off the rest.

"Now I really can't get up." Bryce

groaned, but it didn't look to Daisy like he planned on moving anytime soon.

"Come on, folks!" Asa Pleasant called for everyone's attention. "It's time for a little friendly competition! Everyone who wants to compete in the sack race, get over here and grab a tater sack."

"I always win this one." Logan sprang up from the ground and held out his hand to Hattie. "Want to try to beat me?"

"Sometimes I want to beat you, all right." Hattie laughed as she said the words. "But not at this. You go on ahead." She waved him on.

"Bryce?" Logan issued a one-word challenge.

"Not after that pie," Bryce refused. "I'll join you in a bit."

"Suit yourself." Logan rushed across the eating area to grab a potato sack.

Daisy's heart clenched at the longing in Jamie's eyes as the other contestants lined up. Some things were stark reminders of what he'd never be able to do. *Maybe we should've brought Nosey along, after all. Leastways then Jamie'd have something to play with while the other children run around.*

"Buddy, I want to ask you something." Bryce distracted them both. "I'm going to need a partner for the wheelbarrow race.

175

What'dya say?"

I want Jamie to feel like a part of the fun, but the wheelbarrow race? Where you hold the person's legs and make them walk on their hands? Jamie has much better control over his hands and arms than his legs, but they still jerk around some. Iff'n he spasms and falls . . .

"See, what you have to do is sit inside the wheelbarrow and tell me to swerve left or right to avoid the logs." Bryce's explanation wasn't what she expected. "You'll have to have sharp eyes, but I know I can count on you. First team across the finish line wins some peppermint sticks."

" 'Es!" Jamie's excited nod made Daisy wish she could think of ways to make him feel as included.

"Let's go tell 'em we want to be one of the teams." Bryce picked Jamie up and threw Daisy a wink before tromping over to talk to Rooster Linden.

"Now maybe it ain't my place to tell you this, but you should know." Hattie leaned close to whisper in Daisy's ear. "Bryce arranged this wheelbarrow race special. He's not jist a good, smart man. He's a thoughtful one. I know he won't never tell you what he done, so I'm tellin' it for him."

Daisy sat for a moment, speechless. *Why*

didn't Bryce tell me hisself? I'm right glad he done this. How am I s'pposed to let him court me when he keeps secrets about how wonderful he is?

"Bryce told me he aims to win." Hattie grinned. "Betwixt you and me, I hope they do. Logan's gotten too puffed up for his own good. Brags he'll win every race he enters. I caught him hopping 'round the barn t'other day, practicing for the three-legged race."

"Well then." Daisy smiled mischievously. "What say we level the playing field?"

CHAPTER 17

"Let's have a quick review. Hold out your left arm. Good. Right? Excellent." Bryce patted Jamie on the back. "Now you say it."

" 'Eft, rite," Jamie recited, holding out the named arm.

"We're up." Bryce set Jamie down in the wheelbarrow, facing forward. "Are you ready to win?"

"Yeah!" Jamie gripped the sides of the wheelbarrow and leaned forward to have a better view of the grass.

"On yore marks. Get set . . ." Rooster roared, "Go!"

Bryce, tensed and ready, took off like a shot.

" 'Eft!" Jamie shouted, and Bryce quickly maneuvered around the block of wood.

"Rite!" Jamie directed. "Rite ag'n!"

Bryce kept pushing, running hard and angling the wheelbarrow tightly. He spotted the Trevor twins out of the corner of his eye, gaining.

" 'Eft, Byce!" Jamie screeched. "No mor! Go!"

Bryce saw Daisy waiting at the finish line, jumping up and down and clapping her hands. He managed a final burst of speed. *For Daisy and Jamie!* He sailed over the finish line.

"We win!" Jamie yelled, flailing his arms joyfully as his mama ran over.

"I saw, Jamie!" Daisy scooped him up and swung him in the air. "You were so fast to see those blocks! I'm proud of you!"

Bryce felt as though he'd grown about ten inches taller, seeing Jamie flushed with victory and Daisy beaming with pride. He drank in the sight of them.

After Rooster and Asa presented Jamie with his peppermint stick prize, the whole holler walked by to congratulate him on his sharp eyes. To Bryce's way of thinking, the day was complete.

But it seemed that Daisy had other plans. When Logan grabbed Bryce for the three-legged race, she and Hattie followed over to the racing field.

"What do you think you're doing?" Logan demanded as Hattie tied herself and Daisy together at the ankle.

"We're joinin' the race. What's it look

like?" Daisy calmly slipped her arm around Hattie's waist to steady herself.

"Oh-ho," Logan guffawed. "Well, if you wanted a close view of me and Bryce winning, you could've waited at the finish line."

Bryce tried to elbow Logan in the ribs to get him to shut his mouth, but he just bumped Logan's arm.

"We'll see about that," Hattie shot back, her eyes alight with challenge as everybody lined up.

On "Go!" Bryce took off for the second time that day. He and Logan loped across the field, but Logan's shorter legs made Bryce abbreviate his stride. "Come on! They're gettin' ahead!" he whispered, doggedly dragging Logan along with him.

"It's not my fault we're lopsided!" Logan huffed.

Hattie and Daisy thumped across the field right past Bryce and Logan. *How can they be so graceful? Look at them go!* Bryce watched with a mixture of admiration and disbelief as the women half-walked, half-hopped to victory.

After he disentangled himself from Logan, he went to congratulate them. Seeing Daisy, face flushed from exertion, eyes sparkling with laughter, made Bryce grin. *I'd gladly lose this race if I can win her in the long run.*

"Bryce?" Logan's voice carried across the barn.

"Up here!" Bryce used the worn ribbon to mark the passage he'd barely finished reading, then closed the Bible. He heard Logan's heavy boots on the loft's ladder before he saw his brother.

"Did I interrupt your devotions?" Logan looked at the Bible at his brother's side.

"It's a good place to stop."

"Good. Listen, I've got to go to Louisville in about two weeks and deliver a big shipment before the weather turns bad." Logan jerked a thumb toward the covered window, where very little sunlight strained through. "Train leaves on a Monday afternoon, and I was wondering whether you wanted to come with me."

Hmm. If I stay, I'll see Daisy more often before the snow comes. If I go, I can take care of a few things. I don't like how Daisy wears Hattie's old cloak. She's sewing Jamie a new winter coat, but he should have some warm gloves, too. Besides, I need runners for a sled. That way Jamie won't have to scooch around in the snow and catch cold.

"Sounds good. There's some stuff I need

to pick up. You think this is the last trip you'll make this year?" Bryce wondered whether he'd have a chance to buy everyone Christmas gifts.

"I don't know." Logan scratched his jaw. "I know snowstorms up here make winter traveling difficult, to say the least. All the same, I'd like to get back once more before Christmas. It'd give Daisy time to make more lace, Otis could turn out a few more checker sets, and Asa could carve more nativity sets — Jack says they're sure to be in demand for Christmas. It's a good time of year for selling, and I want to see everybody make the best of it."

"So long as you don't put yourself at risk to make a few more dollars," Bryce warned. "I don't want to see you set out with a full load of merchandise when you can't see ten feet in front of you."

"I wouldn't do that." Logan instinctively looked toward the cabin, although all he could see was the walls of the barn. Bryce knew he was thinking about Hattie. "I don't want to be stuck away from my wife."

"She's good for you," Bryce stated. "You've made a fine choice, Logan."

"Don't I know it!" Logan shot him a grin. "Seems like you're following in my foot-steps. I heard tell that Daisy's glad you're staying."

"Mm." Bryce shrugged, knowing his brother was fishing for answers.

"If you're going to clam up, I'm not taking you to Louisville," Logan prodded. "Especially after you slept practically the whole way to Salt Lick Holler when we left Chance Ranch!"

Bryce threw back his head and laughed. "I wondered how long it would be before your patience ran out, Logan. I have to say, it took longer than it used to."

"Stop trying to get my goat and spill it." Logan punched him on the arm.

"I'm staying to court Daisy. She knows it, and she's agreeable." Bryce folded his arms across his chest. "We're taking things slow, seeing how it works out. No pressure and no promises." *Yet.*

"Did we ferget anything?" Miz Willow fretted from the back of the buckboard a week later. The day's corn shucking would keep them all busy.

"Nope." Bryce turned from hoisting Jamie onto the buckboard and spanned his hands on Daisy's waist. "I've got everything I need."

Daisy could feel the heat spread from her cheeks to the tips of her ears as he lifted her up beside her son. She expected him to go around and take the reins, but instead he jumped in the back and sat next to her. Logan lifted Hattie to sit with him on the seat. She caught Logan sending Bryce a wink, and Daisy knew Bryce and Logan had planned it this way.

They think they're so doggone clever. I see straight through it, but I'll play along. Hattie knows what they're up to, same as me. It's almost endearing.

What're folks gonna think when they see us like this? It's so strange having a man sitting this close, knowing we're courting. Takes me back to when I was a young gal out on hayrides. Bryce is offerin' me a fresh start, and I want to see where the road leads.

The trip to the Trevor place went by fast, and before Daisy knew it, they'd arrived at the corn shucking. Today they'd get through the Trevor harvest, and Asa Pleasant was bringing his over by the wagonload. With everybody in the holler showing up, the work should be done by the end of the day — leaving enough time for a nice lunch and a few friendly games.

"Everybody settle in!" Asa and Ed had already set up the working area. Piles of corn sat ready around every seat. Daisy sat Jamie with the other young children, where he could help, but stayed close. Bryce took the seat next to her, making her the recipient of several scowls from unwed young ladies.

"You all know the rules. Shuck fast and well, and we'll finish real quick. Find a red ear and you get to kiss anyone of yore choosin'." Ed whispered something in Asa's ear, and Asa held up his hands. "Wait a minute. It seems as though last time around we had a few folks not abidin' by the spirit of the rule. No kissin' yore kin anymore, lessen 'tis yore husband or wife. Now get shuckin'!"

No! Daisy briefly closed her eyes. *Iff'n I cain't give Jamie a kiss on the forehead, I'll be in a real fix. This here's whatcha call an impossible situation. Lord, please don't let me find a red ear!*

She worked rapidly, tearing the green leaves off the cobs and pulling away the fine corn silk. People chitchatted back and forth as they worked, and Daisy was glad Bryce didn't require a lot of conversation. They kept shucking in companionable silence for a good hour or so before someone found the first red ear.

"I got one!" One of the Trevor twins waved a red cob in the air, and everyone stopped to watch.

"All right, son." Ed slapped him on the back. "Who's the lucky lady?"

Daisy watched Ted as he swaggered around the circle importantly before stopping. As the young man looked at Nessie, Daisy could've sworn she saw both of them flush. Nessie had already been married once. Her husband ran off on her, and after he'd been gone almost two years, she'd received word that he'd died.

Interesting. So one of the Trevor twins fancies Nessie. She's a good gal; she deserves to have a second husband after what she went through with the first. I wonder, since he'd run off so long ago, should Nessie have to observe a year's mourning? He'd already been missing longer'n that, after all.

Daisy kept her thoughts to herself. Truth to tell, it wasn't any of her business. She didn't like the idea of folks speculating about her and Bryce, though she knew it was unavoidable. *Hopefully we cain keep it casual-like for a while yet.*

Lost in her thoughts, Daisy hadn't realized how quiet it'd gotten. She looked down at the ear of corn she'd shucked out of pure habit. The contrary thing glowed red, and she was the last one to notice.

Oh no! What do I do? I ain't s'posed to kiss Jamie. I cain't kiss Bryce! He stared at her steadily, and Daisy felt like a fool. *Why not? We're courtin' now. So what if folks jabber on about it?*

She held the red ear up in the air before turning to Bryce. Daisy gave him a small smile and leaned in to kiss his cheek. Even though he'd shaved that morning, a slight shadow rasped against her lips, making them tingle at the contact. Up this close, she could smell the faintly spicy scent of his aftershave. She closed her eyes and breathed in his closeness before drawing away.

Bryce looked at her, smiling only enough to show that he was pleased. To everyone watching, he seemed glad to have been chosen but not ruffled by it. But Daisy saw a different story in his gaze. Those blue eyes gleamed with the grin he wouldn't show off, filling the moment with fire and promise.

A few catcalls and some applause sounded out as they always did, but Daisy didn't mind at all. *Let them think what they will. I care for Bryce, and he cares for me. It wasn't a public spectacle, jist a show of affection.*

With the most nerve-racking challenge of the day behind her, Daisy relaxed. The trees wore shades of gold and auburn as the autumn sun shone down upon them. Jamie's movements, alongside those of the other young children, didn't appear too jerky.

They all struggled to shuck a few ears of corn, uncovering more giggles than anything else.

"I done got one!" Lily Cleary waved a red ear in the air, chin lifted in triumph. Daisy watched with interest. Lily had been no more'n a child when Daisy moved to Hawk's Fall. Was there a young gentleman she had her eye on? As the girl purposely made her way around the circle, Daisy thought she knew who it was.

I wonder which twin Lily fancies. Shore hope it's the one as didn't kiss Nessie. It's always nice when things work out like —

Daisy felt her jaw drop as Lily stopped in front of Bryce.

What?

CHAPTER 18

Not me. Not me. Not me. Please keep walking, Lily. Bryce resisted the urge to lean back and howl in frustration as Lily Cleary, no doubt egged on by her mother, put her hands on his shoulders, leaning close for a kiss — a kiss on the lips that lasted far, far too long in Bryce's estimation. When Lily let go, Bryce wiped the back of his neck, wishing he could wipe his mouth. Then he snuck a glance at Daisy.

He'd seen her eyes widen in shock when Lily stopped in front of him, but now her face was blank. *Should I be relieved that she's not upset or disappointed? It would help things if Lily would go back to her mama, so I could think about how to fix this.* Bryce looked at Daisy to see if her expression had changed. *Nope. But wait. Something about the set of her jaw . . .*

Daisy's clenching her teeth! She's not unaffected by Lily's ploy. Bryce bit back a grin.

He'd rather ease a little pang of jealousy than try to create emotion where none resided. He remembered her tentative kiss, Daisy's soft lips lightly grazing his cheek. *She kissed me, and she's not happy that Lily did, too.*

Well, don't you worry, sweetheart. Bryce tried to send the message without speaking. He didn't want to embarrass her. *There's only one woman I'm staying in Salt Lick Holler for.* Something in his face must've reassured her, because her jaw loosened, and she gave him a barely perceptible nod. *Then we understand each other. It's a good start.*

The day passed, the piles of unshucked corn growing smaller while the corncribs strained to hold their bounty. Everybody took a leisurely lunch before getting back to the work at hand. A plentiful harvest this year meant that the fun and games would be postponed.

A short while later, Otis Nye stood up. "Got to stretch these ole legs of mine," he muttered. "Rheumatiz."

Bryce didn't pay him much mind until cheers erupted from the crowd. He looked up to find out what all the fuss was about.

Otis Nye straightened up from bussing Miz Willow's cheek. He wore a self-satisfied grin on his craggy face as he walked back to his seat and reached for another ear of corn.

Miz Willow blushed scarlet, eyes wide in surprise. She lifted her hand to touch her cheek before she realized everybody was watching. "What's so interestin'? Get back to work." She grabbed more corn and got to shucking. For the rest of the afternoon, everyone snuck glances at wily old Otis Nye, but he stayed put as the day wore on.

"I gots another one!" Lily Cleary crowed, looking straight at Bryce.

Oh, no you don't, Bryce glowered. *Don't even think about trying that again. No matter how much your mama pushes you toward me, it won't do any good. I've already found a woman.*

"Lily Cleary, you set back down this minute." Miz Willow's voice cracked through the circle with the force of a whip. "I done saw yore mama pass you that there corn. Shame on the both of you."

"Cain't get anything past Miz Willow!" someone called out.

"How cain you say such a thang, Willomena?" Bethilda Cleary puffed up like a riled peahen.

"I cain say it 'cuz I seen it." Miz Willow didn't give an inch, and Bryce's affection for the old woman grew. *She's a fine woman, that Willomena Hendrick.*

"Don't get all het up, Bethilda." Ed Trevor intervened with a jaunty step. "Fair's fair. It's yore corn, and you do the kissin'."

A sour look crossed Bethilda Cleary's face as she sought out her husband.

"Good to see you, darlin'!" Ed Cleary waggled his brows at his wife as she stood on tiptoe. He swiftly turned his head so her demure peck on the cheek became a full-blown buss on the lips.

"Ed!" Bethilda blushed scarlet and scurried back to her daughters, but she no longer wore a frown. It was obvious that she cared more for her husband than she liked to let on. Ed's mischief had relieved the tension in the air and gotten a chuckle at his wife's foibles.

Bryce laughed along with everyone else but started working double-time. The day was almost over, and he had a goal to reach. *Come on, one of these things has to be red. . . .*

"I've decided not to go to Louisville, Logan," Bryce announced a week later.

"Why not, Bryce?"

"Bad timing. If I go to Louisville with you," Bryce reasoned, "I'll be missing the last days before snowfall."

"That's right." A knowing look passed

across Logan's face. "I should've guessed you'd want to be here with Daisy."

"And Jamie."

"How's that little wagon coming along? Nate Rucker make those wheels like he promised?"

"Yep. He slipped them to me at the corn shucking. I'll have it finished this afternoon." Bryce paused. "We'll take it with us to the church social."

"Good idea. Jamie's on the scrawny side for a boy his age, but he's still almost five. He's getting too big for the women to be carrying him around."

"It should be a good solution for now." Bryce pulled a scrap of foolscap from his pocket. "But when the snow comes, the wagon won't work. I'm planning on making a sled for him. Since I'm not going to Louisville, I'll need to have you pick up a few things." He handed the paper to his brother.

"Runners, rope, wood glue . . . makes sense. I'll see what I can do." Logan squinted at the list. "What's all this other stuff for?"

"Daisy's making Jamie a winter coat, but he'll need gloves, since he uses his hands to get around the cabin. Daisy doesn't have winter clothing, so I want you to get her a ready-made heavy cloak and a wool dress — somethin' fancy, like with stripes."

"I don't know anything about dresses." Logan shook his head.

"Come on, Logan. I had Hattie write down Daisy's size so the clerk can help you. The cloak can be simple — light brown, like a newborn fawn, oughtta do it."

Bryce watched Logan frown and shake his head some more. *Time for a new approach.* "Listen, Logan. We can rope, ride, herd cattle, mend fences, judge horseflesh, shoot straight, work with our hands, play a mean game of horseshoes — are you tryin' to tell me you can't buy one little old dress?"

"Of course I can." Logan jutted out his chin and stalked out of the barn. "But I don't have to like it."

Bryce chuckled and went back to the tack room. He whistled as he fitted the wagon handle to its boxy frame. He'd made it small enough so it wouldn't be unwieldy but large enough so Jamie wouldn't outgrow it any-time soon. Tightening a few pieces, he heard light footsteps.

Without enough time to fling a covering over the wagon, Bryce barreled out of the tack room, all but running straight into Daisy.

"Bryce!" She took a step back to steady

herself. "What's the rush?"

"Uh . . ." Bryce cleared his throat. "I was on my way to see if you wanted to go for a walk during Jamie's nap." He cringed at the fib. Truth was, he did want to ask her that very thing but hadn't planned to go for a few more minutes, at least.

"That's mighty nice of you." Daisy's smile tugged at his heart. "I was jist goin' to ask if you wanted to go for a ride."

"Sounds good," Bryce agreed, then panicked when she stepped toward the tack room. "But a walk sounds better." He snagged her arm.

"It's been a long time since I rode around the hills, Bryce." Her quiet plea melted him. "Soon it'll be winter, and then I cain't."

"All right. I'll go get the saddles. Why don't you . . ." He paused, unable to think of anything.

"I'll get a few sugar lumps for the horses." Daisy slid past him into the tack room and stopped short at the sight of the wagon. "What's that?"

"A wagon I made for Jamie." Bryce hastened to explain why he hadn't wanted her to see it. "It's not quite finished yet."

"It's . . ." Daisy ran her fingertips along the side of the wagon, reaching out to pick up the handle. She gave an experimental tug, and it rolled forward. Bryce held his breath, waiting for her pronouncement. "Wonderful."

"I'm glad you like it."

"Yore so thoughtful!" Daisy turned and gave him a hug. "Jamie will love this, and I'll have an easier time takin' him around. Thankee, Bryce."

She looked up at him, her brown eyes glowing with gratitude. Her lips hovered so close. . . .

"You're —" Bryce groaned and closed the distance between them, holding her against him as he touched his lips to hers. *Gentle, soft . . .*

After they both drew away, Bryce touched his forehead to hers. "Wonderful."

CHAPTER 19

Daisy shoveled ashes from the stove belly into the ash pail.

Wonderful. She touched her lips, reliving Bryce's kiss. Had it only been two weeks since he decided to stay? How quickly she'd come to see him as more than a friend. He was so strong, gentle, tender, rough . . . *Bryce.*

The puppy's cold nose bumped against her elbow insistently, causing her to scatter a few ashes onto the floor. "Nosey!" Daisy put down the shovel and cuddled the animal close.

The tiny pup served as yet another reminder of how thoughtfully Bryce attended to the needs of her son. Daisy rubbed Nosey's silky fur once more before setting her down. The pup immediately scrabbled toward Jamie, nails clicking on the hardwood floors.

" 'Ook!" Jamie held up his slate for her

inspection. There, in the big, loopy letters of her son's hand, rested one word. *L-o-v-e.*

"Oh, Jamie!" Daisy knelt down and pulled him into a hug. "That's some mighty fine work. It does yore mama's heart good to see you so smart."

" 'Ove you," Jamie crooned, giving her an awkward pat on the shoulder.

"I love you, too, baby." Daisy drew away so Jamie could keep working. As Nosey stuck her snout on the slate, giving it a wet imprint of approval, Daisy smiled. *Jamie and I love each other. And Bryce loves us both.*

"Hello in there!" Bryce's voice called from the yard.

"Yes, Bryce?" Daisy flung open the door.

"Can Jamie and Nosey come out to play?" His voice sang with mischief and fun.

"Jist a minute!" Daisy waited for Jamie to get a firm hold on the puppy before carrying them both outside.

"Hi, Byce!" Jamie positively sparkled whenever they spent time together.

"Hey, buddy. Got something for you."

"Wut?"

"This!" Bryce whipped the cover off the wagon he'd made just for her son.

"Wow!" Jamie wiggled with excitement, and Nosey let out a few celebratory yaps.

198

"What say your mama and I take you and Nosey for a ride?" Bryce suggested, wheeling the wagon closer.

"Pease?" Jamie looked at her with wide eyes.

"Of course!" Daisy laughed and deposited him in his wagon. He still clutched Nosey, who kept very busy snuffling the sides of the wagon.

Bryce nestled a blanket in the bottom so Jamie would be more comfortable and steady. *He's so good at adapting things to make others feel comfortable.*

Bryce pulled the wagon smoothly along the path while Daisy walked alongside. Jamie squealed with glee when Bryce began making wiggly zigzags. They didn't go too far — just enough to know that the arrangement would work.

Seems to me that with Bryce around, a lot of things are better'n afore. Mayhap the wagon isn't the only thing that will work between us.

"Now let me see. . . ." Bryce rubbed his jaw and stared at the wagon. With Logan gone to Louisville, he had the time to take Jamie fishing before it got too cold. "I've got Jamie — you've got Nosey?"

" 'Es!" Jamie held up the wiggly pooch

before tucking her back in his lap. Nosey fared well with Jamie's attention and the cow's milk Bryce kept feeding her.

"I've got the poles and tackle box. You have that lunch basket your ma packed?"

Jamie nodded and patted the basket. It rested in front of him in the wagon.

"Sounds like we're ready to go catch some supper!" Bryce took hold of the wagon handle with his free hand and set off. "The fish know the weather's changing, so we should have no trouble coaxing a few onto the line."

Jamie played with Nosey as Bryce pulled the wagon along the dirt road. He stopped when he spotted a shady patch of moist earth. He turned the wagon onto the grass, where it jounced along more roughly.

"Whee!" Jamie held on tight but looked around in confusion when Bryce stopped. " 'Ish?"

"Before we catch fish, we'll need bait." Bryce lifted the youngster out of the wagon and sat him down. He pulled out his pocketknife and dug up some of the dark dirt. "I need your help. We have to dig around until we find worms!"

"Mess." Jamie looked at the dirt longingly.

"This is man's work. Your mama knows we'll get a little dirty." Bryce scooped some of the dirt into Jamie's fingers and un-earthed a pink worm. He grabbed it and dropped it into the jar he'd brought along. "See? Now let's get a bunch more."

Jamie didn't need to be told twice. The small boy burrowed into the earth with gusto, scattering dirt everywhere. Nosey watched for a minute before joining in, her front paws scrabbling to widen the hole. The little boy held up his filthy fist, eyes shining in glee. "Got't!"

"Good one." Bryce held out the jar, and Jamie dropped in a fat earthworm.

It didn't take long for Bryce to judge they had enough. He picked up Jamie, turned him upside down, and gave him a few light bounces. The lad giggled as specks of dirt rained to the ground. Nosey gave herself an emphatic shake, starting at her nose and wiggling all the way down.

"Let's go to the stream." Bryce got them both situated in the wagon — Jamie insisted on holding the jar of worms — and made their way to the fishing hole. Bryce splashed Jamie's hands with water before they shared a picnic lunch of egg-salad sandwiches and coleslaw. Then it was time to get down to business.

"Eeww!" Jamie shrieked, fascinated as Bryce laced the first worm onto his hook.

"Here." Bryce cast the line into the water and handed the small, lightweight pole to Jamie. "Hold it tight, and let me know when you get a bite."

"How I know?" Jamie stared at the pole blankly.

"It'll move." Bryce reached out and gave the line a gentle tug. "Like that. Then you tell me, and we'll haul in your fish. Remember, you have to be as quiet as you can."

" 'Kay!" His little brow furrowed as he concentrated on the task at hand.

Bryce baited his own hook, then hunkered down beside Jamie. The little boy couldn't really hold the pole steady, but he did a good job trying. They sat in silence, listening to the rippling water and the whisper of the wind through the long grasses at the water's edge. Birdcalls rarely disturbed the quiet, since most of them had flown south already.

"Byce!" Jamie gripped his pole tightly, trying to steady the wobble.

It took Bryce a moment to decide if it was Jamie shaking or a fish on the line. Bryce scooped Jamie up and put his hands over the little boy's to steady them. The line danced in the water. He immediately started walking back, drawing the line from the water until a fair-sized fish flopped on the bank. Bryce pulled it farther from the water so it wouldn't slide back.

Nosey trailed the slippery fish from the water's edge, backing away when its tail hit her in the muzzle. The little dog looked up at Bryce and Jamie, wagging her tail as though to say, "We did it!"

"Would you look at that?" Bryce sat Jamie down before sliding the hook from the fish's mouth. "First fish of the day. Way to go, buddy!" He handed it to Jamie and pushed the water pail closer. "Go ahead and put it in the bucket of water."

Jamie dropped his catch into the pail, beaming with pride. "Ag'n?" he asked hopefully.

Bryce nodded and handed him the pole, ready with a worm dangling from the hook. "We've got a whole pail to fill. Let's get to it so we've got enough for supper when we go back home."

Winter came in a flurry of snow and ice, blanketing the ground in a single night. Daisy woke up to see her own breath and rushed to put more wood on the stove. She dressed Jamie in the flannel long underwear she'd scarce finished for him, layering his pants and shirt atop so he'd keep warm. His woolen winter coat hung ready on the

hook by the door iff'n she took him outside
at all.

*Don't see no reason to risk it. Jamie gets
along jist fine even though he cain't use his
legs, but in the snow he'll get drenched and
icy cold so quick. His wagon won't pull him
through snowdrifts. Iff'n he catches cold,
Jamie ain't strong enough to fight it off like
most boys.*

Daisy shredded the potatoes, pushing the
knife into the roots hard as she thought
about how frail her son's health could be.
*It'll grow into pneumony, and I'll lose him. Best
keep him inside. Bryce'll still take him to the
barn to visit the animals, and Jamie has
Nosey in here. It'll have to do.*

The fried potatoes and coffee steamed on
the stove when Logan and Hattie walked
through the adjoining door and said good
morning to Miz Willow, who didn't look up
from reading her morning devotions. Bryce
fetched Jamie to gather the eggs, then
brought the basket back full. Hattie helped
Daisy scramble them up with chunks of
ham.

"First snow of the winter!" Logan grinned
as he downed his breakfast.

"Beautiful out there," Hattie agreed.
"Snow turns the world into soft white
curves, like givin' it a clean coat of white-

wash, only better."

"I can't wait. Fresh-fallen snow has so many possibilities." Bryce turned to Jamie. "You have your long underwear on, buddy?"

"Yep!" Jamie pulled on the neck of his shirt to show Bryce the red flannel beneath.

Now why would Bryce ask a question like that? He's not planning on taking Jamie out in the snow!

Alarmed, Daisy stared at Bryce.

"Snow angels are a must," he said, going right on with his planning. "Maybe a snowman, too."

"Not today, fellers." Daisy rose and cleared the empty platters.

"Why not?" Logan demanded.

"I haven't made Jamie his gloves yet, so he cain't go out in the snow." *There. That's a solid reason. It'll even take me awhile to make the gloves. Iff'n I stretch it out, I might not have 'em done afore blizzarding season. Then he'll hardly use 'em a'tall.*

"That reminds me." Bryce fumbled in his pockets and pulled out a pair of small blue woolen gloves with a matching scarf. "Seems as though I missed your birthday, Jamie. Just a month before we met." Bryce shook his head. "I had to do something to fix that!"

Daisy drew a deep breath as he fit the gloves onto Jamie's tiny hands before wrapping the scarf around his neck. Her son held his hands out in front of him and wiggled his fingers gleefully. The gloves Logan had picked up for him in Louisville fit perfectly.

"Ready!"

"What about yore lessuns?" she burst out, desperate to keep Jamie out of the cold.

"It's the first snowfall, Daisy!" Logan pushed aside her protest like it was nothing more than a pesky gnat.

"But Jamie don't have a second pair of flannels," Daisy protested. "Iff'n those get soaked through, he'll get cold."

"We'll have warm towels waiting in the oven to dry him off before he changes," Bryce reassured her as he helped Jamie into his coat and put on his own, too. "And I'm sure you'll have some hot tea waiting, too. It'll be fine."

With that, he whisked her son out into the snow, the door banging shut behind them.

"I said no! Why won't they let me raise Jamie as I see fit?" Daisy paced around the cabin. "He cain't catch cold. It's too dangerous!"

"I know." Hattie began fixing some tea. "But I'll have those towels warm, and we'll get him some tea. He's bundled up out there, too. I reckon a boy's got to play in the snow sometime, Daisy. Might as well be now."

No, it shouldn't.

CHAPTER 20

"This way." Logan lay down in a fresh drift of powder and spread his outstretched arms and legs open and shut. "That's how you make a snow angel!"

Bryce put Jamie down and grabbed his shoes to move his legs in the proper motion. The boy waved his arms up and down in imitation of Logan. Bryce lifted him back up so he could survey his handiwork.

"Ange's!" Jamie pointed excitedly at the impression he'd made in the white blanket covering the earth.

"And a very fine one it is, too," Bryce assessed. He put Jamie down in his wagon. Sure, it wouldn't roll through the drifts, but it was a dry place for Jamie to sit down. Hattie had spoken with him about Jamie's health. He wasn't strong enough to handle a cold like most kids. It'd turn to pneumonia and take his life. Bryce needed to be extra careful.

All the same, it did no good protecting Jamie's life if no one let him live it. The boy deserved to enjoy all the wonder of childhood. Bryce intended to give him all the laughter and adventure possible during the time they had.

"We're going to teach you how to make snowballs." Bryce put a lump of the soft ice in Jamie's hand, took one for himself, and demonstrated how to mold it into a round ball.

"Once you're done, put it down and start a pile. Keep making more." Bryce, Logan, and Jamie all worked to make dozens of snowballs.

"I've got an idea." Logan started carrying some and putting them in a heap beside the cabin door.

"What are you up to?" Bryce had a funny feeling it involved getting Hattie and Daisy to play in the snow.

"You'll see." Logan came back and hunched on Jamie's other side. "Hattie! Daisy! Grab your cloaks and come out here for a minute!"

The door opened, and Hattie stepped outside in her pink-hooded cover. "What is it?"

"Snowball fight!" Logan lobbed one at her shoulder.

"No fair! We're unarmed!" Daisy glowered at Bryce.

"Snowbaws!" Jamie pitched one, but it fell short with a soft thud.

"To your left, ladies!" Bryce waited for them to throw the first volley before reciprocating. Then the fight was on.

He held Jamie's hand and helped him swing his arm, showing him when to release the snowball so it would go farther. The little boy learned quickly, hitting Hattie and Daisy more times than Bryce thought possible. Their carefully created supply of ammunition dwindled rapidly.

"That's it. We're out." Bryce stood up. He heard the whoosh too late to duck and ended up with a collar full of melting snow. "Who did that?"

"Me!" Daisy stood like a warrior, framed in the doorway she'd built with him. Her cheeks glowed a pretty pink, a smile stretched across her rosy lips, and she gripped one last snowball in her left hand.

"We surrender! We've got nothing left!" Logan put his hands up.

"Nothing doin'!" Hattie swiped Daisy's final snowball to toss at her husband. It smashed into his chest, and Logan sank to his knees.

"Brought down by my own wife!" he

moaned. "Right in the heart!"

"Quit yore bellyachin'!" Miz Willow shook her cane at them. "You called the girls out for a snowball fight and came off the worse for it. You got nobody to blame 'cept yoreselves. Come inside and warm up afore you catch your death out here."

Daisy stayed outside after Hattie and Logan tromped into the cabin, waiting for Bryce to hand over Jamie. As Bryce saw her cuddle her son, burrowing her face into his hair, he felt warm despite the cold. He, Daisy, and Jamie would make a good family. All he had to do was bide his time until Daisy realized the same thing.

"Daisy," Miz Willow began as she laid down the pad of paper with numbers scrawled across it. "You know you don't have to do this. We got plenty of room here."

"Don't get me wrong, Miz Willow. Yore place is mighty fine, and I cain't tell you how much I 'preciate yore hospitality." Daisy searched for the words. "But Hawk's Fall . . . Peter bought that land when we first wed. It's home to Jamie an' me."

"Darlin', I know it was. But that house is gone forever." Miz Willow's observation tore at Daisy's heart. "Even iff'n you could scrimp enough to rebuild, it wouldn't be what holds yore memories."

"I ken that. But the land is all we got left now." Daisy drew a deep breath. "So I need for us to keep on goin'." *Logan, Jamie, and Bryce won't stay out in the barn for'ver, and Hattie'll be back from the Pleasant place soon.* She managed a tight smile as Miz Willow picked up the paper and pen once more. "You got how much per piece? Now we need to figgur out how many veils, runners, and collars you cain make per year."

"It takes a powerful long time to make lace, so . . ." Daisy thought long and hard before she gave the answer.

Miz Willow's pen scratched across the paper as she laboriously added it all up. "How much did Logan tell you the lumber would run? Hearth bricks? The workers?" The old woman frowned at the numbers she wrote. "You take into account all the thangs you'll need? Furniture, pots, pans, stock of dry goods, blankets, hearth rug, buckets, hay for yore mule, and such?"

"Not yet." Daisy lifted her chin in determination. "We'll get by on whatever's left after food and clothes for Jamie an' me." She rattled off still more numbers Logan had helped her figure out.

"That's it, Daisy." Miz Willow sucked in a sharp breath. "You only got but two dollars left. Ain't nearly enough to outfit a home, even iff'n you manage to make as much lace as you say you cain this winter."

Daisy's throat closed. *It's not enough. I cain't possibly make any more lace than that, and even with the extry money from Logan's trade deal, it won't suffice. Why? I work so hard. It should be sufficient to provide for Jamie and me. I've always managed afore. I'll think of somethin'.*

"Iff'n I swaller m' pride an' ask Logan and the men 'round here to holp me out" — Daisy shut her eyes at the thought of asking for charity — "so's I don't pay for the work, would it be enough?" *It has to be.*

Miz Willow squinted at the pad. "I don't reckon it would, Daisy. Even if the men of the community pitch in like they should and build the house and even yore furniture for you, you'll jist have enough left to buy wood for next winter and keep yore mule in hay. Yore still missin' blankets, pots, pans, and such like."

"I'll work harder," Daisy spoke quickly, desperately. "How 'bout iff'n I make two more collars this winter?" *I'll work into the nights. Somehow, I'll get it done.*

"Not quite." Miz Willow shook her white locks. "It'd almost be enough, but yore for-gettin' how you an' Jamie need winter thangs. Yore already makin' him a coat, but that's jist a start."

"I don't need anythin'. I got Hattie's ole cloak. I'll get by." Daisy straightened her shoulders with resolve.

"What about candles?" Miz Willow pressed her. "And Nosey?"

I cain't ask Jamie to give up his pup. She sleeps curled up aside him at night, follows him durin' the day. Daisy buried her head in her hands and willed herself not to give in to the sobs rising in her throat. *No matter how hard I work, I cain't do it. There's not enough time to take care of Jamie and make enough lace to rebuild our home.*

Her chest hitched, then tightened. Daisy's breath grew ragged. Panic welled inside her. *I cain't provide for my son.* She took in quick, shallow breaths, not getting enough air.

"Here." Miz Willow thrust a cup of tea in her hands. "The steam oughtta holp you breathe. I'll go get some eucalyptus oil." She rushed to the storeroom and back, dotting something beneath Daisy's nose. "Take slow, deep breaths now, else yore gonna faint." Miz Willow squeezed her hand. "And you might as well let out them tears. They've been a long time comin'."

The wail rose from the bottom of her soul as Daisy gave in. Hot tears rushed down her face, her shoulders shaking with the intensity of her sobs. Miz Willow held her as she cried for Peter, for Jamie, for the loss of their home, for knowing she couldn't keep everything together no matter how hard she tried. When there was nothing left inside her, she straightened up and used the third handkerchief Miz Willow passed to her.

"What am I gonna do?"

"First thang is to calm down, now that you've let it all out." Miz Willow briskly took the cooled tea from the table. "Then take a moment to realize yore already done with the hardest part."

"What?" To Daisy's way of thinking, the hardest part lay ahead.

"You admitted you need holp. That's somethin' you've been avoidin' for a far sight too long."

Mayhap, Daisy admitted. *But now I have to ask for the holp I need.*

"So now that yore facin' the facts, I figgur you've got two paths you cain take." Miz Willow pinned her with a no-nonsense gaze. "You an' Jamie are more'n welcome in this house. Yore son brightens my day, and yore a bigger holp 'round here than you know."

"Thankee, Miz Willow." Daisy swallowed the lump of pride lodged in her throat. "It's a good place to raise Jamie."

"Yore welcome, Daisy. I ain't jist returnin' the customary response to thankee, neither. I want you to listen and pay me heed. You and Jamie are welcome here. Yore wanted and loved, and all of us know how hard you work. You'll still be providin' for yore son, jist under this roof where you cain holp me, too. Understand?"

"Yes, ma'am." Daisy's heart softened toward the old woman. *She's a good woman and teaches Jamie useful thangs, too. Truth of the matter is, Jamie's gettin' bigger, but no better at carin' for hisself. I need more holp with him, and having Hattie and Miz Willow around puts me more at ease on account of them bein' healers. The wood floor is nice for Jamie, too. We cain have a good life here.*

"Now that we've got that settled, I'm going to put a fly in the ointment." Miz Willow's rocker began to creak rhythmically. "Seems to me yore overlooking Bryce. He's dead set on marryin' you. You've encouraged his courtin'. How cain you be so set on rebuildin' in Hawk's Fall iff'n yore givin' any thought to marryin' agin?"

"It's early stages yet." Daisy bristled. "I cain't see into the future, and I got to be ready."

"Say you two do marry up. His ranch is

out in Californy. Have you given any thought to movin' out there?"

"I'd be lyin' iff'n I tole you the thought hadn't crossed my mind," Daisy admitted.

I cain't imagine leavin' these hills. My whole life's fit into the valleys and peaks. The cricks and crags of this land hold memories and reminders. A woman follows her man — that's why I left Salt Lick for Hawk's Fall. But it's only half-a-day's ride. Californy's clear cross the country.

"Are you willin' to pack up Jamie and leave?" Miz Willow prodded further. "Otherwise, you should tell Bryce now."

"Iff'n he offers for my hand, and I accept, it'll be with the intention of going where he leads." Daisy spoke the words aloud for the first time. "Even if it is all the way to Californy."

"Good." Miz Willow stopped rocking to lean forward. "Lovejoy writes that it's a fine place. You'll have four sisters-in-law and lots of nieces and nephews for Jamie to play with. Weather over there'll be easier on him, too. Logan's sitting pretty from his share of the ranch, and Bryce'll be jist as well off. The Chance men are good workers. He'll take care of you and Jamie so's you needn't fret no more."

"That ain't any type of reason to enter

217

into marriage. I don't aim to wed Bryce so's he'll put a roof o'er my head," Daisy denied firmly. *Iff'n we wed, it'll be for love — 'cuz we don't want to part. We'll become a family together — not a burden Bryce has to work to maintain.*

"Jamie's my responsibility. I cain't rely on Bryce to provide for us."

CHAPTER 21

Bryce froze at the certainty in Daisy's tone. He'd just left Jamie in the barn to towel off some of the dried mud from Nosey's fur, meaning to ask the women if they needed him to get anything from the smokehouse for supper.

"I cain't rely on Bryce to provide for us." The words knocked the air from his chest, and he exhaled sharply. Bryce stepped away from the cabin, unwilling to hear any more.

Jesus, help me! No matter how I twist the words, I can't make anything good out of them. She said outright that she can't rely on me to provide for her and Jamie. How can she think I won't provide for them? She knows about Chance Ranch. Daisy's seen me build rooms, barns, wagons. She has to know I'm more than capable of taking care of my own. There's only one thing those words can mean. I've done everything I can think of to show her that I'll take good care of her and her son.

What more can I do?

Bryce trudged through the snow until trickles of water ran into his boots. He stopped pacing and shook his head to clear his thoughts.

Can it be money? Does Daisy think I'm destitute? I sleep in the barn because this isn't my home. I haven't showered her with courting gifts because I didn't want to raise her hackles. She hates thinking she's charity, and I wouldn't make her feel low for the world. So how do I tell Daisy I'm more than solvent? It's not exactly the type of thing you mention in conversation.

Bryce began pacing again.

Words won't do it. If I'm going to show her I am a good provider, I'll have to think of something else. I'll go to Louisville with Logan this last time before Christmas and buy up anything and everything I think she and Jamie would want. If she doesn't think of it as charity but as tokens of affection, it won't affront her. I'll prove that I'm financially stable.

Having determined a course of action, Bryce stomped back to the barn, shaking snow off his boots.

Lord, thank You for letting me overhear Daisy's concerns. Now that I know she's worried about finances, I can put those fears to rest. I don't know how she got the idea that

Chance Ranch isn't prosperous and I might not be able to provide for her and Jamie, but it's a mistake I can set right. When I'm done, she won't have a doubt in her mind that I will be a good provider for our family.

"Good thing the snow's light today," Daisy observed, trudging through the slush with Hattie.

"Otis Nye's place ain't far, but we couldn't make it the past few days on account of the snowstorm. His rheumatiz acts up somethin' dreadful in the cold. He'll be needin' more devil's claw tea." Hattie pulled her cloak tight against the frosty air, and Daisy followed suit.

"That cloak shore do look nice on you, Daisy." Her motion must've drawn Hattie's eye. " 'Twas good of Bryce to think of it."

"I never felt wool so soft." Daisy stroked the fawn-colored fabric. "It don't set right the way Bryce done give me this cloak and Jamie his scarf and gloves, while I ain't done nothin' in return."

"Don't be a goose, Daisy," Hattie harrumphed. "They's courtin' gifts. Fine choices, too."

"Bryce is good about findin' out our needs and fillin' 'em," Daisy had to admit. "It shore is nice to have a man pay me mind like that."

"Well, you pay attention right back. Don't think I haven't noticed how many apple pies and such you've been bakin', Daisy Thales!"

"Cookin's the only thang I cain do right now to repay his kindness. Courtin's betwixt two people, and I ain't 'bout to let him do all the givin'."

"We all know you ain't like that, Daisy." Hattie shot her a disgruntled look. "That winter coat you sewed for Bryce is dreadful fine."

"I ain't quite finished with the linin'." Daisy wanted the gift to be perfect. "It'll be ready for Christmas."

"I cain't believe he's made it through all this time with jist that one light coat." Hattie shook her head in wonder. "Mayhap 'tisn't my place to go runnin' my mouth, but Bryce shorely has gone outta his way to court you."

"I don't think there's any way left for him to show me how serious he is." Daisy paused. "Makes me feel . . ." *Beholden.* She pushed away the negative thought. Bryce made her feel so much more than that. *Wanted. Taken care of.* "Special."

"I hope so. A man don't stay through one of these winters sleeping in the barn unless he's dead set on gettin' his woman," Hattie observed. "Good reminder that money ain't ev'rything. It's God who provides for us in ev'ry way." She shook her head. "I cain't believe Bryce thought to buy you a cloak and plumb fergot to get one for hisself. Shows 'zactly where his mind is."

Yes. His mind is set on me and Jamie, and my heart's yearning for Bryce to return. He's been gone to Louisville less'n a week, and I miss him. When he gets home, I know this'll be a Christmas to remember.

"You think this'll fit her?" Bryce held up a green-striped wool dress.

"I dunno." Logan eyed him thoughtfully. "Put it up against yourself so I can see if it'll be too long or not. Daisy's a lot shorter'n you are."

Bryce gave a resigned sigh and held the ruffled collar under his chin. The end of the dress barely brushed his knees. "What's the verdict?"

Logan couldn't keep a straight face. "Makes you look almost dainty!" He let loose a few hearty guffaws.

Bryce rolled his eyes and handed the dress to the shopkeeper, along with Hattie's measurements of Daisy. "Will this fit?"

The man took out a measuring tape and

busily checked the length and other dimensions. "Like a glove."

"Wrap it up," Bryce ordered. "Wait a minute. Do you have gloves?" He ignored Logan's loud groan as he surveyed a selection of ladies' hand wear, picking out a daytime pair of blinding white cotton before a heavy winter pair of black wool.

He laid the gloves in his palm, remembering the feel of Daisy's hand in his, so tiny and delicate. "These'll do." He passed them to the clerk.

"Is there something else you're looking for, sir?"

"What would you suggest in the way of robes?" Bryce had thought long and hard before figuring out what to get for Hattie and Miz Willow.

"A robe?" Logan echoed. "Don't you think you're going a little far, Bryce?"

"Nope. I'm getting one each for Hattie, Miz Willow, and Daisy. Folks come knocking on their door at all hours of the night, so they need dressing gowns. If I get one for each of them, no one will be affronted."

"That's a good idea," Logan murmured enviously. He started prowling around the shop, looking with renewed interest at the wares lining the shelves.

"These velvet dressing gowns are popular." The young clerk led him over to a display. "Any color in particular?"

"Purple for Miz Willow, pink for Hattie," Bryce decided. He fingered a deep forest green robe with white flowers embroidered on the edges. "This one for Daisy."

"These, too." Bryce pointed to a set of tortoiseshell hair combs lying in a case. Their gleaming brown color would make Daisy's honey curls shine even brighter. *I'll give these to her as soon as we get back to Salt Lick Holler. The other things can wait a few days for Christmas.*

"Very good, sir." The clerk's smile grew broader with each item he rang up.

Bryce eyed the growing pile, not yet satisfied. *There must be something else I can think of to get her. I have to prove that I've got the wherewithal to care for her and her son. Too much is riding on this to let it be, but what am I forgetting?*

"If I might be so bold," the clerk suggested, "we have a lovely selection of shawls to your left."

Bryce inched closer, picking out a cream-colored shawl whose delicate color and weave put him in mind of Daisy's lace. "I'll take this, too."

"An excellent choice." The clerk carefully folded the shawl and laid it atop Bryce's large pile of items.

Almost. Is there anything she'd really like? Something special that wouldn't do for any woman but just for Daisy?

"Do you carry things for women's toilettes?" Bryce knew he'd mispronounced the last word, but the shopkeeper nodded and showed him to the far corner. Bryce looked over the vanity sets, recalling how strongly Daisy felt that a woman should have a looking glass in her home. When he flipped over one of the handheld mirrors, he found a single daisy etched into the silver plating on the back. *Perfect.*

"It belongs to a set, sir." The clerk industriously laid out a matching brush, comb, and some other strange implement.

"What's this?" Bryce picked the thing up to scrutinize it.

"A nail buffer. I'm certain your wife would like it." The clerk lifted the silver buffer from its tray as he explained.

"She's not my wife," Bryce corrected. "Yet."

Daisy slid another batch of cinnamon rolls into the oven before tending to her hair. She slipped the tresses from their nightly braid and combed through the entire mass before pinning back half of her hair and letting the rest fall free. For the finishing touch, she slid the beautiful tortoiseshell hair combs in place.

"Jist right." Miz Willow nodded her approval at Bryce's homecoming gift.

He'd taken her aside right after he and Logan got back to push a small bundle in her hands. "I missed you," he'd whispered in a husky voice that made her heart sing.

"I missed you, too." Daisy had kissed him on the cheek before opening the bundle and finding the dainty hair combs. "You didn't need to do this!"

He'd laid her head on his shoulder, holding her close to his heart. "I wanted to."

So on Christmas morning, three days later, she wore them for the first time. Mistletoe and holly decorated the cabin in celebration of the Savior's birth. Boughs crackled in the stove, sending the woodsy scent of pine to mingle with the cinnamon and yeast of the rolls. The cabin smelled of cherished memories and surprises yet to come.

After a hearty breakfast, they got ready to leave for church.

"Here, Daisy." Bryce held out her cloak for her. "Beautiful." He reached out to touch one of the combs, running his fingers through her hair.

227

"They are." Daisy smiled.

"I didn't mean the combs." Bryce's compliment made her heart thump faster as they made their way to the Christmas service.

CHAPTER 22

Heart full to bursting, Daisy sang the familiar Christmas hymns fervently. *"Oh, come, all ye faithful, joyful and triumphant. . . ."*

I feel joyful and triumphant. Today, long ago, Christ came into the world to save us all. Here and now, I'm surrounded by the people I love. What more could I want?

They transitioned into her favorite carol. *"Silent night, holy night. All is calm, all is bright. . . ."*

Everything is calm, soothed by love that makes the world shine bright. I've done it. Jamie and me got through the fire and hard times, and now I cain make shore he's taken care of. I've got it all under control.

The circuit preacher cleared his throat from the makeshift pulpit.

"Today, on the birthday of our Savior, I'm planning to deviate from the normal Christmas service. Instead of reading the Gospel's account of Christ's birth, it's on my heart to focus on what Jesus meant to accomplish by the mortal life He took on."

What? Well, I s'pose it's all right. We cain read it together at home. I wonder what he's drivin' at?

"We're coming to the end of the year of our Lord 1874, and as another year has passed, I want each of you to think back on how you've spent your days. I'll give you a moment to think on it."

Losing a house, working hard to care for Jamie, and finding a home and mayhap even true love. Daisy couldn't help but be satisfied with her answer.

"If you're honest, you'll realize you thought of a lot of things you're proud of, and maybe a few you aren't so proud of." The preacher paused to let his words sink in. "Now don't raise your hands. This isn't between anybody but you and the Lord. How many of you thought of works you'd done?"

Of course I did. Daisy shifted restlessly. *Jamie and me's been through a lot this year, and it's taken a lot of work and determination to get through it.*

"How many of you thought about how you'd grown in your faith?" The preacher pressed on. "How you've been blessed in your walk with the Lord?"

No. I reckon I've been a mite busy of late.

"Have you been relying on yourselves and the things you do to get by, or have you put your faith in the providing hand of the Lord?"

I've been working. Iff'n it were jist me, I'd have the luxury of doin' thangs different.

"Well, today, on Christmas morn, I want to remind each and every person here why Christ came to earth. To save you and me and everyone who loves Him. No matter how busy we are, how much we do with the time we're given on this earth, we can't save ourselves."

A pang shot through Daisy's chest.

"We are saved through faith alone." The preacher's voice grew stronger. "Second Timothy 1:9 reminds us that Christ is He 'who hath saved us, and called us with an holy calling, not according to our works, but according to his own purpose and grace.' " The preacher laid down his Bible and faced them.

"We cannot take with us the things we work for here. We are saved through faith in the Lord Jesus Christ, who is the one and only way, truth, and life. Remember that as you go today. Put the Lord first and give Him your all. He already did as much for each of us."

Conviction surged in Daisy's breast. *I ain't been leaning on the Lord as much as I should, but I'll remember to do better in the future. I ain't even prayed about my feelings for Bryce! I've been trying to control my life when it ain't my own. I gave it to Jesus long ago, and I need to do a better job of trusting Him with it.*

Lord, I'm sorry for turning away from You. I been caught up in works and pride instead of love and faith. Thank You for all the blessings You give me — Jamie and Bryce foremost among them. Lord, I've fallen for Bryce Chance. Iff'n it be Yore will that he take me to wife, I'd be a happy woman. I leave it in Yore hands, and wait in faith for Yore will to be done. Amen.

"Good sermon," Bryce commented as they made their way back home for Christmas dinner.

"Yes." Daisy's tone made him look at her. Consternation warred with relief as she spoke again. "Made me realize I been tryin' too hard to control everything in me and Jamie's lives instead of leanin' on my Lord. Somethin' that weren't pleasant to see, but I needed to face it."

"Good." Bryce smiled at her. "God made you a strong woman, Daisy, but He didn't make you to go through life alone. He's at

232

your side every step of the way, even when you don't let Him carry some of your burden for you."

"I know." Her eyes shone with joy. "He sent you."

Bryce kissed her on the cheek. As his lips grazed her soft skin, he whispered a prayer of thanks.

Lord, that's the closest she's come to admitting she returns my feelings. Please let today show her I'm an able provider and put her fears to rest. Thank You for working in her heart so she knows she doesn't have to be strong alone.

As they gathered around the table, Bryce read Luke 2, telling of the Savior's birth: " 'And, lo, the angel of the Lord . . . said unto them, Fear not: for, behold, I bring you good tidings of great joy, which shall be to all people. For unto you is born this day in the city of David a Saviour, which is Christ the Lord. And this shall be a sign unto you; Ye shall find the babe wrapped in swaddling clothes, lying in a manger.' "

The words washed over him, comforting and familiar while filling him with awe. *God gave up all His power to come to earth as a mortal child. He lived, loved, and taught the people around Him before allowing Himself to be sacrificed for us. Jesus Christ, Son of God, gave Himself to save us from our sins.*

"Lord," Logan prayed when Bryce finished the passage, "we thank You this day for coming to earth long ago as a child, living as a man, and dying for our sins. Your birth was a miracle; Your sacrifice amazes us. Having taken our sins upon Yourself, You rose again to create a place for us beside You in heaven. We thank You for all You've done for us. Amen."

As they ate the meal, Bryce drank in the love surrounding him. They came together to celebrate the Lord, and in doing so celebrated the life He'd given them. When the last dish was cleared away, they brought out the gifts, sharing with one another all Christ had given them.

Bryce watched in anticipation as everyone opened their packages.

"This is wonderful, Hattie! Thank you!" Miz Willow held up a box of fancy paper stationery. "I'll use it when we write to Lovejoy and our family at Chance Ranch."

Bryce didn't miss the sly look the old woman sent him. *Yes, Miz Willow. If I have my way, you'll be writing to Daisy and Jamie, too.*

"Look at this!" Hattie pulled on her pink dressing gown as Miz Willow opened hers. "Thankee, Bryce!"

"Thought they could come in handy," he explained.

"They should, what with folks droppin' by at all hours for the healer." Miz Willow patted the purple velvet with satisfaction. "Nice and cozy, too."

"Oh!" Daisy drew out her green dressing gown, touching the little white flowers embroidered on the collar. "How pretty!"

"Those flowers put me in mind o' daisies," Hattie praised. "What a clever gift!"

"Thankee, Bryce." Daisy's happy smile made him feel about ten feet tall.

"You're welcome, Daisy." He took the package she passed him.

"This is from me and Jamie."

"A coat!" Bryce put it on immediately. "I've been needing one of these. Now I'm glad I didn't pick one up. This is the finest coat I ever put on!" He rubbed his hand on his wool sleeve. "Nice and warm."

"I made it myself." Daisy beamed at his appreciation.

" 'Ook!" Jamie lifted the pair of long underwear Daisy'd sewn him. "For sno'!"

"That's right." Daisy rumpled her son's hair affectionately. "So you have some after you play in the snow."

"Here, buddy." Bryce handed Jamie two packages, one after another.

Jamie attacked the paper, ripping it haphazardly until he uncovered a spinning top. "What is't?" He held up the toy and gave it a curious glance.

"A top." Bryce reached for it and set it on the ground. "This is how you use it." He gave the top a spin, and the brightly painted toy whirled around the floor. Nosey followed the whirling thing until it tipped over, then nudged it back to Jamie.

"Wow!" Jamie picked it up. "T'anks!"

"Go on and open the other one," Bryce urged. He grinned at Daisy as Jamie unearthed a miniature cowboy hat just like the ones he and Logan wore.

Jamie plunked it on his head. "See?" He craned his neck toward Daisy, who smiled.

"You look jist like a cowboy, Jamie."

Bryce nodded at her words. That was the whole idea. Every boy who lived on a ranch needed a cowboy hat.

"Oh, Bryce." Daisy stared at the vanity set nestled in tissue paper. *How did he know I always wanted a vanity set? This one's so pretty, too. Brush, comb, mirror.* She gasped as she picked up the mirror and spotted the etching on the back. She traced the shape of a daisy with her fingertips. "It's perfect." She looked at Bryce. "Where did you ever find this?"

"Sometimes it's worth the search to find something special."

He thinks I'm special and I deserve special things. Bryce's words put a lump in her throat. *Lord, he's already given me so much.*

"This is beautiful, Daisy!" Hattie held up the long, thin piece of lace Daisy'd woven to serve as a bookmark.

"I'm glad you like it." She smiled.

"I'll use mine in my Bible." Miz Willow admired hers. "Such a fine piece of work. Little touches of beauty to enrich the heart."

Logan had gotten matching flannel nightgowns — one for his wife and one apiece for Miz Willow and Daisy. He and Hattie also gave Jamie a warm flannel nightshirt.

I have so much to be thankful for.

As the day wore on, Daisy's smile began to fade. *Is it possible to have too much to be thankful for?* Piles of presents from Bryce surrounded her. In addition to the vanity set and velvet dressing gown, she'd received no less than two pairs of gloves, a delicate cream-colored shawl, and a store-bought wool dress with green piping. She'd never owned any store-bought clothing before the cloak Bryce had given her at the beginning of the winter.

Jamie sat beside her on his brand-new

beginner saddle, cowboy hat perched atop his head slightly askew as he bent over to spin his top. So many expensive things. Suddenly, Daisy remembered the combs in her hair, and the gloves and scarf Bryce had already gotten Jamie.

It's too much! I'd never be able to buy half of all this if I worked my fingers to the bones for years! Why did Bryce get so carried away? How can I let him know how I feel without angering him? He meant well, but Jamie and I aren't charity! The coat I made him seems so paltry now, and he's still wearing it as though it's the grandest thing he's ever received.

Daisy got up and busied herself with picking up bits of brown paper and twine, putting them in a bucket to burn later. Needing a moment to herself, she decided to tote Jamie's saddle to the barn.

"I'll take that." Bryce smoothly slid the saddle from her arms and walked beside her.

Daisy didn't say a word, her thoughts all a jumble.

Bryce hung the saddle on the rail beside his own and turned to her. "Something wrong? I'll be careful teaching Jamie to ride."

"It's not that —" Daisy broke off.

"What is it?" He stepped closer to rub her shoulders.

"Stop it." She backed away. "Why did you get all those thangs for us, Bryce?"

"Didn't you like them?" Consternation painted his face.

"Of course. They're all wonderful thangs, Bryce," she hastened to reassure him. "But they're so much."

"I want to give you everything in the world, Daisy." He tried to draw close again, but she put out her palm.

"We ain't charity, Bryce." Tears of frustration filled her eyes.

"I never thought you were." He held her hand, brushing his thumb across her palm. "Truth is, I want something in return." His eyes burned with meaning, sending a blaze of heat running up her spine.

"You don't buy love, Bryce." He dropped her hand like it was a hot potato, but she had to make him understand. "I never wanted yore money."

CHAPTER 23

Bryce stared at the woman he'd come to love so desperately, trying to understand what it was she wanted from him. *If you didn't have qualms about finances, then what —*

The only other possible explanation hit him like a punch in the gut. *She meant she can't rely on me. Won't trust me to take care of her and her son. Daisy's grown so used to making her own decisions that she won't give up control for the compromise of marriage.*

He realized Daisy was staring at him, waiting for him to explain why he'd showered her and Jamie with tokens of his love.

What do I say to her? How can I tell her what I overheard and ask her to explain? How can I not?

Bryce decided to lay it all on the line. "On the day Logan and I took Jamie sledding for the first time, I came back a little before the others." His throat grew hoarse as he told her. "I heard what you said to Miz Willow."

He watched as Daisy began turning bright pink with embarrassment.

What, 'zactly, did he hear? Daisy frantically tried to remember the conversation. *Did he hear me and Miz Willow talkin' 'bout movin' to Californy? Is he angry that we even dared presume such a thang? Did he think I was trying to take advantage of his wealth?* Her heart constricted. Best to approach this with caution.

"A woman has to think about these things," she hedged. Bryce's eyes darkened further, and she swallowed. *Why cain't I say the right thang jist this once?*

"So there's no other explanation?" His voice sounded toneless, muted, and flat.

"We're courting seriously now, Bryce," Daisy begged him to understand. "It's a lot to consider. I have to think about Jamie."

"I see." A muscle in his jaw ticked. "And what did I ever do to lead you to think that?"

Oh no. He doesn't want to take me and Jamie back to Californy. It's his home. It's where he planned on going anyway, but we never talked about it. I jist assumed that's what he had in mind when he said he was goin' to court me. Her spine stiffened. *If I got that wrong, what else have I missed?*

241

"You said you were staying to court me." Daisy planted her hands on her hips. "You promised you'd treat Jamie as if he were yore own. What was I supposed to think?"

"That I don't make promises I can't keep." Bryce's eyes snapped blue fire at her.

"So that's why we never talked about it?" Daisy fumed. *He weren't makin' any promises on account of him not wanting to take us back to Chance Ranch. Why? Is he ashamed of us?* A chill shot down her spine. *Is he ashamed of Jamie? Is that why he don't want us to meet his kin?*

"I thought you knew!" Bryce growled. "You're a smart woman, Daisy Thales. How could you think for even a moment that I would propose marriage to a woman with a son without —"

"Without what, Bryce?" she interrupted. "Without making shore you wouldn't have to be ashamed of us in front of yore kin?" Daisy blinked back tears for the second time that day. "How could I have been so foolish? You bought all those thangs to fancy me up because I'm too plain and not book learned. You don't think me and Jamie are good enough to take to Californy!" She whirled around.

She didn't make it through the door before he grabbed her arm, forcing her to stop and face him.

"Let me go!"

"No!" he roared, pulling her closer. "Don't you understand that I've done everything I have so I wouldn't have to ever let you go?"

The anger and passion throbbing in his voice made Daisy stop trying to get away.

"What makes you think I could ever be ashamed of you? You're an amazing woman. I've pursued you every way I could think of so you'd be my wife." Bryce stopped shouting and looked at her in sorrow and disappointment. "How could you believe I'd be ashamed of you or Jamie? What? Because he can't use his legs? It doesn't matter to me, Daisy. I love Jamie like my own son."

"Then why are you so mad that Miz Willow and me talked about me and Jamie moving to Californy?" Her voice came out sounding small and sad, but she couldn't do anything about it.

Lord, I'm so confused. I hurt. Please holp me.

"What?" Bryce's brow knit in confusion. "I heard you say something else." He took a deep breath as though about to repeat something painful. "You told Miz Willow you couldn't rely on me to provide for you and Jamie."

"I never —" Daisy broke off as she recalled

the very end of that conversation. "No. I didn't mean them words. You —"

"Heard them." Bryce stated flatly, cutting her off. "I thought you meant you weren't sure I had the money."

That's why he bought all those thangs — he was tryin' to prove he was a good provider! Daisy felt the faint stirrings of hope.

"Bryce, I know you're a good provider and a fine man. I seen you work with my own two eyes!"

"And now I know you don't 'want my money.' " Bryce's eyes glinted in pain. "I know that you weren't talking about how you thought I didn't have the means to support you."

"No! I never thought that at all!" Daisy argued excitedly.

"So you meant you couldn't trust me." Bryce shook his head. "If you don't believe me when I tell you I want to take care of you and Jamie," Bryce kept speaking as he pushed past her, "then there's nothing left to say."

Bryce stopped in midstep as Daisy grabbed him by the back of the collar.

"Yore not goin' another step till I've had my say." Her fury all but steamed out of her as he turned around.

"Fine." He crossed his arms in front of his chest and waited. *But we both know there's nothing you can tell me that'll change the problem.* His heart ached. *You're still not willing to share your life. Daisy, you won't even give control over to the Lord. So long as you rely on yourself, we're not spiritually suited. It's over.*

"You cain't jist catch the tail end of a conversation and assume you know all there is to know." Daisy put her fisted hands on her hips and stared up at him. "For yore information, Miz Willow had said summat about how well-off you and Logan was, and how you'd take care of me and Jamie. What you heard me say was the end of my response."

Bryce listened closely as Daisy gave a deep sigh. "I tole her that a roof ain't no reason to marry up. Iff'n we got married, it would be for love and nothin' else. Jamie's my responsibility, and I wouldn't marry you to ease my load."

Bryce took a moment to realize what she meant. *She doesn't want me for my money. It's not that she doesn't trust me. She just wanted to enter into the courtship with a pure heart so love could grow. How could I have been so wrong?*

"Daisy!" He enveloped her in his arms

245

and clung tight. "I misunderstood."

"It's all right." She wiped her teary eyes. "Yore not the only one guilty of that."

"I thought you were still relying on yourself for everything, not giving control to God."

"I meant what I said this mornin', Bryce," Daisy spoke earnestly. "I've been wrapped up in my own works, and that cain't stand. Now I'm willing to trust in God's will."

"That's a big step." Bryce stroked her hair.

"And even though we misunderstood one another, I trust you, Bryce. I know I cain rely on you."

Bryce tipped her chin up and gave her a kiss. "Then I can't think of anything that could stand between us."

Bryce hoisted Jamie up into the saddle, then looped a length of rope around the boy and secured the other end to the pommel. "This'll help keep you on her back," he explained. "Now hold onto the pommel — this knobby thing on your saddle — with both hands while I adjust your stirrups."

Winter's snowstorms hadn't abated, so they'd only go up and down the barn a few times. Perfect for Jamie's first riding lesson.

"Now take your right hand and grab the reins," Bryce instructed, making certain

Jamie had a good grip on both the reins and the pommel. "When you want to go forward, flick this up and down, leaning forward just a little. When you need to stop, you pull back. Remember to be gentle so you don't hurt your mount." Bryce went to the horse's head and took hold of the halter to guide her. "Ready?"

"Ready!" Jamie leaned forward and shook the reins. The horse took a few steps forward, ambling slowly.

Bryce watched Jamie hold on tight as the horse swayed side to side while moving straight ahead. "You're doing fine, buddy," Bryce called. "This is what we call a walk. When you've had some more practice, and we have you outside where there's enough room, we'll move up to a trot."

"What t'ot?" Jamie asked, yanking back the reins as they came to the end of the barn.

"Gentle, remember?" Bryce gave a quick reminder on how to pull to a stop without hurting the horse. "A trot is a fast walk. You know how you're shifting a little from side to side as you go forward?" He waited for Jamie's nod to continue the lesson. "When you go faster, in a trot, you'll go up and down a bit, too."

"Oh." Jamie nodded solemnly. The little

boy concentrated hard as they went up and down the barn a few more times.

Bryce waited until after they'd seen to the horse and gotten it settled back in its stall. Then he brought up the subject he'd been biding his time for.

"Jamie?"

"Yep?"

"You know that I like your ma, right?"

"She 'ike you, too." Jamie nodded, eyes big.

"And we both like you." Bryce tickled Jamie's tummy, making the little boy squeal with laughter.

"I live in California," Bryce continued. "I was wondering if you and your ma might go back with me."

"Cal'fa?" Jamie struggled with the state name. "Wher'?"

"A long ways away. That's why I want you and your ma to come with me," Bryce explained. "It's the only way I'll see you anymore."

"Don' go," Jamie instructed. "Stay."

"I have to go back. My family and my home are out there. If you and your mama were there, too, I wouldn't be missing anything. We'd all be together, and you could meet my nieces and nephews. Some of them are about your age, so you could play together."

Jamie frowned as he pondered this. "Wiwwo?"

"Miz Willow would stay here," Bryce answered honestly.

"Oh." Jamie scrunched up his face. "Why me an' Ma go?"

"I want your permission to ask your mama to marry me. She'd be my wife, and then you'd be my son. I'd be your second pa." Bryce held his breath and waited for the answer. He wanted to have Jamie's agreement before he proposed to Daisy. They were supposed to become a family.

"Pa?" Jamie's eyes lit up, and his face broke into a grin.

"So I can ask your mama to marry me, and we can all go to California?" Bryce asked.

" 'Es!"

"Good, because I need your help."

"Where's Bryce?" Daisy kept looking at the door every few minutes. "He was only going to put away the sled."

"Jamie and I'll go check up on him." Logan stood up importantly, picked Jamie up, and tromped out the door.

When Logan and Jamie didn't come back, either, Hattie and Daisy put on their cloaks to see what was going on.

"Jamie!" Daisy called. "Bryce?"

"Over here!" She and Hattie walked around the barn, following the voice.

"Stay right there!" Logan ordered.

"What's —" Daisy's words were cut off by a mighty *whoosh* as a sled came flying down the snowbank, stopping less than two feet from where she stood.

"Hi!" Jamie, all bundled up in his scarf and cowboy hat, waved his arms from where he sat, sandwiched in front of Bryce on the biggest sled Daisy had ever clapped eyes on.

"We've got a good team going here." Bryce grinned at her. "But I think we've got room for one more."

"I'm not getting on that thing!" Daisy refused. "No matter how much room is on it!"

"Well, not until we get it to the top of the hill, at least." Bryce handed Jamie to her. "Meet me at the top."

Left with no choice, Daisy trudged up the snowy hill. "Bryce, I . . ." The words died in her throat as she looked around her.

"Surprise!" Jamie clapped excitedly as Daisy walked over to the sight before her.

A blue tablecloth covered an old tree stump. Bryce stood beside it, taking her hand and helping her step over the roots. He helped her sit down, Jamie resting on her lap.

"What are you up to, Bryce Chance?" she asked.

"We're waiting for a friend." Bryce pointed over to where Nosey trundled through the snow, determined to reach Jamie. When the dog, no longer a tiny puppy, reached them, Bryce picked her up.

"Nosey has something for you." He held the growing puppy up, and when Daisy reached out to pet the animal, she noticed a piece of twine tied around Nosey's neck.

"What's this?" She fingered the thick string. Nosey didn't need a collar, since she hardly ever left Jamie's side.

"Pull it in and find out," Bryce prompted. Daisy grabbed the long end of the string and began pulling.

And pulling, and pulling. Jamie giggled with glee as she brought up more and more twine. *What have they got on the end of this thang?*

Daisy gasped as she caught sight of the sparkling ring. Nosey snuffled her hand in wet encouragement as Daisy grabbed it.

"Daisy." Bryce dropped to one knee, still holding Nosey under one arm. "We've got quite a little group here. I've spoken with

Jamie man-to-man and gotten his blessing to ask you something." He reached for her left hand, looking deep into her eyes. "Will you be my wife and make us a family?"

Daisy could only nod while Bryce slid the engagement band onto her finger. "Yes!" She finally managed. She stood up, and Bryce gathered her and Jamie into his warm embrace. *I might not stay in Salt Lick Holler,* Daisy knew, *but I've found my home.*

"Got a surprise for you two back at the cabin," Logan announced a few minutes later as he rocked back and forth on the balls of his feet.

"Oh?" Bryce wondered what his brother'd done this time.

"When you told me how you'd be proposing, I made a few arrangements of my own." Logan grimaced as Hattie elbowed him in the ribs. "*We* made a few arrangements."

They all marched back to the cabin, Daisy shooting Bryce quizzical looks.

"I have no idea what they've planned." Bryce squeezed her hand.

"Preacher Jacobs!" Daisy's gasp told Bryce what was afoot. Logan and Hattie had made arrangements for the preacher to stop by while he was still in town.

"Are you ready for this, Daisy?" Bryce

cupped her face in his palms. "We can wait if you want."

"Why wait?" Daisy's eyes sparkled up at him. "I love you and want to be yore wife."

His heart soared at her decision. "Let's be wed now then."

"Not quite yet." Miz Willow shooed Hattie and Daisy into the adjoining room. "You have to give the bride a moment to ready herself."

Bryce waited with Logan, Jamie, and the preacher.

"What's taking so long?" Logan paced around the cabin impatiently. Any stranger would've thought he was the one getting married.

"Hold still," Bryce ordered. "Daisy's worth the wait." *Always has been.*

She stepped out of the room in her green-striped wool dress, one of her delicate lace collars framing her face. She wore the gloves and hair combs he'd given her, too. Bryce swelled with pride at the sight of her.

He scarcely heard the words spoken by the preacher, although he knew the vows by heart. When the time came for him to pledge his love, his voice sounded gruff to his own ears.

"With this ring, I thee wed." Daisy sounded ethereal, like sunshine dancing on the grass.

"I now pronounce you man and wife," the preacher intoned grandly. "You may —"

Bryce kissed his bride.

"Good-bye, dearie." Miz Willow gave Jamie and Daisy one final hug. The snow had cleared enough for them to travel back to Chance Ranch.

" 'Bye!" Jamie chirped. He patted his cowboy hat more firmly in place. " 'Bye!"

Hattie stood on tiptoe to give Bryce a farewell hug. "I know you'll take good care of them," she whispered to him. "Give my love to Lovejoy."

"I'll be sure to," Bryce pledged. He turned as Logan slapped him on the back.

"Can't believe you're going." Bryce's younger brother shook his head. "Tell everybody I miss them, but I'm happy." Logan stopped to smile at Hattie. "Thanks for coming to Salt Lick with me, Bryce." Logan gave him a quick nod before almost cracking Bryce's back in a big bear hug. "Be happy."

"I will." Bryce smiled at Daisy and Jamie. "I will." After their final good-byes, they boarded the train and leaned out the windows to wave as Hawk's Fall, Logan, Hattie, and Miz Willow faded out of sight.

"I'm going to miss them." Daisy sniffed.

"I know." Bryce slung an arm around her shoulder and rubbed her arm. "Me, too. But you're going to have a whole army of people waiting to meet you back at Chance Ranch."

"That reminds me." Daisy nestled Jamie into the seat next to her. "I still don't know their names."

"Well, I'll run through them with you. You won't be able to call my brothers by name until you've been around them awhile. We all look a lot alike." Bryce rubbed his jaw.

"No, you don't," Daisy said loyally. "I could tell you and Logan apart the first time I met you."

"I appreciate that I caught your eye right off the bat," Bryce teased, "but it won't be so easy when there are five Chance brothers around. I had to come clear to Kentucky to catch your eye."

"You'll always hold my attention, no matter how many relations are on that ranch of yores." Daisy laid a hand on his chest. "I've already got me the Chance of a lifetime."

ABOUT THE AUTHOR

Kelly Eileen Hake is the daughter of Cathy Marie Hake, and she lives in southern California. Kelly Eileen is pursuing an English degree to share her passions with a new generation.

The employees of Thorndike Press hope you have enjoyed this Large Print book. All our Thorndike and Wheeler Large Print titles are designed for easy reading, and all our books are made to last. Other Thorndike Press Large Print books are available at your library, through selected bookstores, or directly from us.

For information about titles, please call:
(800) 223-1244

or visit our Web site at:
http://gale.cengage.com/thorndike

To share your comments, please write:
Publisher
Thorndike Press
295 Kennedy Memorial Drive
Waterville, ME 04901